DEAD MAN'S PUZZLE

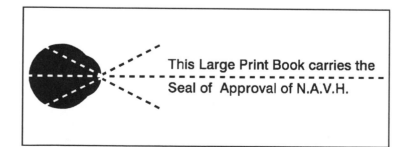

This Large Print Book carries the
Seal of Approval of N.A.V.H.

A PUZZLE LADY MYSTERY

DEAD MAN'S PUZZLE

PARNELL HALL

THORNDIKE PRESS

A part of Gale, Cengage Learning

GALE
CENGAGE Learning·

Detroit • New York • San Francisco • New Haven, Conn • Waterville, Maine • London

LIBRARY OF CONGRESS CATALOGING-IN-PUBLICATION DATA

Hall, Parnell.
 Dead man's puzzle / by Parnell Hall.
     p. cm. — (Thorndike Press large print mystery) (A Puzzle Lady mystery)
 ISBN-13: 978-1-4104-1703-9 (alk. paper)
 ISBN-10: 1-4104-1703-4 (alk. paper)
 1. Felton, Cora (Fictitious character)—Fiction. 2. Crossword puzzle makers—Fiction. 3. Crossword puzzles—Fiction. 4. Large type books. I. Title. II. Series: Hall, Parnell. Puzzle Lady mystery.
 PS3558.A37327D38 2009b
 813'.54—dc22   2009017231

Published in 2009 by arrangement with St. Martin's Press, LLC.

Printed in the United States of America
1 2 3 4 5 6 7 13 12 11 10 09

For Lynn,
who knows computers

THE USUAL SUSPECTS

I would like to thank Will Shortz, *New York Times* crossword puzzle editor, NPR puzzle-master, star of the movie *Wordplay,* and editor and presenter of his own series of enormously popular sudoku books, for creating a sudoku to cheer up Cora. With Sherry off on her honeymoon, Cora was lonely and needed something to boost her spirits. A challenging sudoku was just the ticket.

I would like to thank Manny Nosowsky, famed constructor and frequent *New York Times* contributor, for creating crossword puzzles to drive Cora crazy. With Sherry off on her honeymoon, Cora, who couldn't solve a crossword puzzle to save her life, was embarrassed by them and forced to tap-dance like crazy.

I would like to thank Ellen Ripstein, national champion of the American Cross-word Puzzle Tournament, for editing the puzzles. It was, as always, a pleasure to pass on the responsibility to her.

Without these three shining stars, this book would not have been possible. I can't thank them enough.

CHAPTER 1

"I'll be fine."

Cora Felton patted her niece's hands and smiled brightly, the trademark Puzzle Lady smile that graced her nationally syndicated crossword puzzle column.

"I know you will," Sherry said. She looked cute as a button in a fossil-colored safari shirt and matching convertible pants, the legs of which zipped off to make shorts. A floppy sun hat and mesh hiking boots completed the picture. "I just want to make sure you've got everything straight."

"You told me before."

"You were watching a soap opera."

"I was multitasking. Good practice. Sharpens the brainpower."

"As I was saying. It's important to get it straight."

"Didn't they call your plane?" Cora said.

"No, they didn't call our plane. Or you wouldn't be here. We haven't gone through security yet."

"Oh, right."

"Now, pay attention."

Cora sighed. "Couldn't you have told me this on the way?"

"You were driving."

"So?"

"I didn't want you to drive off the road."

"You think I can't drive and talk?"

"I know you can drive and talk. Drive and listen is another matter."

"I see what you're doing. You're trying to be such a pain I won't miss you."

"When you get back to the house and don't know what to do, you'll be glad we had this little talk."

Sherry Carter and Aaron Grant were leaving on their honeymoon. After a long and fitful courtship, they had finally tied the knot. Cora always knew they would; still, it had been touch and go, what with Sherry's abusive ex-husband, Dennis Pride, always poking around and Aaron's former girlfriend Becky Baldwin on hand. It had happened at last, and the young couple were off to Africa to track the migration of the wildebeest. Cora shuddered at the thought. She wasn't entirely sure what a wildebeest was, but she doubted there was a man in the world attractive enough to induce her to track one.

"The Puzzle Lady columns for the next two weeks are ready to go. Each set is paper-clipped together with a Post-it with the date." Sherry cocked her head like a school-teacher. "Is that the date the puzzle appears in the paper?"

"Is it?"

"No!" Sherry cried in exasperation. "It is the date you are to fax the puzzle. And where is the number you are to fax the puzzle to?"

"I may have missed one or two things," Cora admitted.

"It's on the cover sheet you're faxing. Each fax you send out consists of three pages. The cover sheet. The puzzle. And the solution. You put them in the fax machine how?"

"I take the paper clip off."

"But in what direction?"

"I put them in the top, they come out the bottom."

"Cora."

"Isn't that right?"

"What's the direction of the pages when you put them in?"

"Does it matter? If they're upside down, they can just turn them around."

"Not top and bottom. Front and back.

The writing side faces away from you. The blank side faces toward you."

"Then how do I read the phone number?"

Aaron came back from checking the departure board. The young reporter looked happy. Whether it was from not having a deadline for two weeks or from marrying her niece, Cora wasn't sure. Aaron wore a similar outfit, carried a backpack.

"Is the plane on time?" Sherry asked.

"Safari, so good," Aaron deadpanned.

"Oh, God, is it too late to get out of marrying this guy?"

"You already did."

"The plane's on time," Aaron said. "We gotta go."

"You kids run along now," Cora said. "I'll be fine."

"What do you do if you have to reach me?" Sherry said.

"I won't."

"In case of emergency."

"In case of emergency, someone would find you."

"In an emergency, I don't want someone spending half a day finding me. I have an international cell phone."

"You do?"

"The number's on my desk. With the rest of the instructions."

12

"See," Cora said. "You're giving me a hard time, and all this is written down."

"If you need me, call me. If you don't get me, leave a message on my voice mail."

"Unless we're out of range," Aaron said. "These things can be out of range."

"In which case you e-mail me," Sherry said.

"You have e-mail?"

"See? You weren't listening at all. You leave my e-mail closed. You leave your e-mail open. You e-mail me here, I pick it up there."

Cora frowned. "You have the same account there?"

"It's not that I have an account there. It's that I can pick it up there."

"How?"

"At Hotmail dot com."

"Sounds like a porn site."

"You can e-mail me, and when I get it, I can either call you or e-mail you back."

"Just have a good time."

"We will."

Cora smiled. She supposed they would.

So would she. Despite. It was sweet of Sherry to worry, but Cora was a big girl. She could take care of herself. After all, it was only for two weeks.

What could possibly go wrong?

CHAPTER 2

Cora Felton slammed the red Toyota into a turn. Leaves shot out from under the wheel. The car skidded slightly, gripped pavement, rocketed down the road. Up ahead, sun filtering through the trees glinted off the tan Lexus as it flashed around the curve out of sight. Cora scowled, ascribed the power of the procreative process to the sun, the trees, and the car. She flipped down the visor, stomped on the accelerator, and hunched over the wheel, preparing to negotiate the tricky S-turn, which seemed to lose a new guard post every year as some unsuspecting driver was ambushed by an icy patch from the first early frost. She handled the S-turn by driving straight through, no problem, unless someone happened to be coming in the other lane. Today no one was. Cora shot through, gained a couple of seconds on her quarry.

Not enough. The Lexus was still a hun-

14

dred yards away and coming up on Dead Man's Curve. Not that anyone had died there, that was just Cora's nickname for it. The turn wasn't hard to negotiate, but it was right before the light. The traffic light that held her fate in the balance. Would it stop the Lexus? Or would it let the Lexus go and stop her? And if it let the Lexus go, would it still be in sight? Or would it be a coin flip which way it had gone? A three-sided coin, actually — right, left, or straight ahead?

As Cora swept through the curve, first the road to the left and then the road straight ahead came into her field of vision. No car. The Lexus had gone right.

The light was red. A New York City girl born and bred, Cora Felton had a New York license, but she seemed to recall the Connecticut right-on-red rule had something to do with coming to a complete stop and making sure there was no traffic before turning. In fact, Dale Harper, the Baker-haven chief of police, had reminded her of that on at least one occasion.

Cora made the turn on two wheels, didn't signal, and cut off a bus. Which wasn't that easy to do in Connecticut. In New York Cora cut off buses all the time. Here it was quite an accomplishment. You had to go out of your way to find one.

Up ahead, the Lexus caught the traffic light just as it was changing.

Cora snorted. Wouldn't you know it. The guy doesn't even know he's being followed and blunders into the perfect escape.

Cora was pretty sure there was no straight-ahead-on-red rule in Connecticut. On the other hand, there was nothing coming in either direction. No reason to stop except for a useless formality designed to serve a purpose at a time of high traffic. This was not that time. The light was serving no purpose whatsoever but to make her lose her quarry.

Like hell.

Cora gunned it through the light, saw no one, offended no one, and hurtled down the road.

The Lexus, which must have been doing a hundred, or at least seemed that way, was heading for another S-curve. Cora stomped on the gas.

A car pulled out of a side road. Cora saw it in the rearview mirror. Paid it no mind. Whoever it was, it wasn't going to keep her from her task. Cora screeched into the S-curve, left it in the dust.

The Lexus was turning right, heading for the mall. That was fine by Cora. It would be good following him through the mall. Give her a chance to hone her skills. If he turned into the mall, she had him.

Cora was gaining ground, but so was the car behind her. That made no sense. Why should anyone be trying to keep up with —

Uh-oh.

That wasn't just any car. It was a police car. A cruiser with a bubble on top. The lights weren't on. Maybe it didn't want her.

It did.

Despite the fact Cora was doing seventy, the police car was closing the distance. Just as the Lexus was slowing and signaling a turn.

Cora was caught like a rat in a trap. About to be squished between the cops and her quarry.

And the cop was Chief Harper.

Well, that sealed it. She'd never live it down. There was only one thing to do.

Feign ignorance.

Cora spun the wheel, fishtailed into the mall parking lot, and screeched to a stop in the parking space that miraculously opened up in front of her.

Her Toyota was still rocking when Chief Harper pulled up behind her.

CHAPTER 3

Cora got out of the car, faced a rather exasperated-looking Chief Harper. "All right," she said, "you got me."

"Didn't you see me behind you?"

"That was you?"

"Yes, that was me. Why didn't you stop?"

"Why didn't you use your siren?"

"I don't use the siren unless I'm making an arrest."

"You're not arresting me?"

"For what?"

"For whatever you're not arresting me for."

"I'm not arresting you for anything."

"I guess that covers it."

Chief Harper frowned, peered at her suspiciously. "You sound like a woman with a guilty conscience."

"Do you know how many times I've been married? Probably not. I lose track myself. Anyway, it's a lot. So I'm used to a guilty conscience. It's practically my default position."

Harper put up his hands. "Please. No wordplay. Which was great, by the way. Why weren't you in that movie?"

"What movie?"

"The crossword puzzle movie. *Wordplay.* With Will Shortz."

"Oh, that."

"Why aren't you in it?"

Cora wasn't in the movie because she'd ducked interviews, failed to return phone calls, and not shown up to film. She was afraid her crossword puzzle expertise, which was nonexistent, would be exposed in such a movie. "Just bad luck, Chief. Well, if there's nothing else . . ."

"Nothing else? I stopped you, for goodness' sakes."

"You did, and you didn't say why. Instead you talked about everything else under the sun. You're like a gossipy old woman. What do you think that is, Chief? ADD? Early Alzheimer's?"

"Okay, let me start over. I was trying to stop you because I need your help."

"Please tell me it's a murder."

"It's not."

"Damn."

"At least, I don't think so."

19

"Why do you say that?"

"He died of natural causes."

"Or so it seems?" Cora said hopefully.

"The man was ninety-two."

"Why didn't you say so? He clearly deserved to die. It's a wonder they didn't take him out and shoot him."

"Mr. Overmeyer had cancer of just about everything."

"Was there an autopsy?"

"Why should there be an autopsy?"

"To see if he met with foul play."

"What makes you think he met with foul play?"

"The fact you're asking me about him. You almost ran me off the road to do it."

"I thought you didn't see me back there."

"Let's not quibble. What do you want?"

Chief Harper took out a paper and unfolded it.

Cora's heart sank.

In spidery handwriting and drawn with shaky pen lines was the most loathsome of all possible things known to mortal man.

A crossword puzzle.

An unsolved crossword puzzle.

A crossword puzzle that needed solving.

1	2	3	4		5	6	7		8	9	10	11	12	13
14					15				16					
17					18			19						
20				21			22					23		
	24					25		26			27			
			28			29		30			31	32	33	
34	35	36	37				38		39					
40					41			42		43				
44			45		46			47						
48				49		50								
		51		52		53			54	55	56			
57	58	59		60		61		62					63	
64		65				66			67					
68					69				70					
71					72				73					

Across

1 October's birthstone
5 Math proof abbr.
8 Marked with smears
14 Westminster hopefuls
15 Press into service
16 Stannum source
17 Creole cooking staple

21

18 Start of a message
20 In a seemly way
22 Open wide in a way
23 Network: Abbr.
24 Just say no
26 El padre's brothers
28 Spanish flowers?
30 A third of an inning to go?
34 Part 2 of message
39 Alarming event
40 Gillette product
41 Name on a 1945 bomber
43 Genghis or Kublai
44 Bite like a bee
46 Part 3 of message
48 C.E.O., e.g.
50 Cash in Cancún
51 "Our Gang" affirmative
53 Low bow
57 Concern of Winchester's "The Professor and the Madman"
60 Ladder rung
62 Navy's goat, e.g.
64 Part 4 of message
67 "Okay, break _____ !"
68 _____ del Fuego
69 "_____ Misérables"
70 Frisbee
71 Mosquito barrier
72 Had a little lamb?

73 Just-prior periods

Down

1   Baseball's Blue Moon
2   Lowball or stud
3   Feel the same way
4   Attorney-to-be's exams
5   Area near a wharf
6   "Is" to Ovid
7   Say it isn't so
8   "I've heard enough from you!"
9   Swimmers in a school
10 Corn or cycle prefix
11 Clinic group
12 Lee side?
13 Hankerings
19 Bran source
21 Pre-euro money in Milano
25 Daffy Duck and others
27 Great, in Variety
29 Nose around
31 Pearl Harbor's island
32 Russian range
33 Care for
34 Cartoonist Thomas
35 "The Simpsons" bus driver
36 It goes before the fall?
37 Folk music accompaniment
38 Nobelist Wiesel et al.

Cora cursed her lucky stars, which clearly weren't doing their job. After all, what were the odds her niece couldn't go away on her honeymoon for two short weeks without a dead body with a crossword puzzle showing up in Bakerhaven? It was a very small town. And a very short time. What were the odds?

Well, at the moment, a hundred percent. Chief Harper had just dropped one in her lap. Granted, the man wasn't murdered; still, a dead body with a puzzle was her least favorite thing. Odd, since a dead body *with-*

out a puzzle was her *most* favorite thing. At least a murdered one. So, take away the puzzle and let the old man turn out to have met with foul play, and it would have been the best of all possible worlds.

Instead, it was a disaster.

Under normal circumstances, Cora would stall Chief Harper, take home a copy of the puzzle, and let Sherry solve it. With Sherry in Africa, it would be hard. Could you text-message a puzzle? Could you solve it over the phone?

Cora knew what Sherry would do. Sherry would scan the puzzle and e-mail it as an attached file. Cora felt proud of herself for knowing that. Unfortunately, she only knew that was what Sherry *would* do. She didn't know how to *do* it. Sherry wouldn't be home for a week. Could she stall Chief Harper that long?

"Are you doing it in your head?" Harper asked.

That snapped Cora back to reality. She was most certainly *not* doing it in her head. "I was trying to concoct a scenario in which this might be of interest to the police. You say the man obviously died of natural causes. Who cares what the crossword puzzle says?"

Harper frowned. "Come on, Cora. That's

not like you. There could be lots of reasons."

"Like what? He was an international spy and knows where Jimmy Hoffa was buried? Somehow I tend to doubt it."

"Me too. But solve it anyway."

"All right," Cora said. "I take it there's no rush. I'm a little busy, what with Sherry and Aaron away."

"Ah, the happy couple. How are they? I was beginning to think those two would never tie the knot."

"No kidding. When I was their age, I'd have snapped the guy up like that. Of course, he isn't rich."

"Were all your husbands rich?"

"When I met them." Cora shrugged. "Except Melvin, of course. Melvin just pretended to be. I should have known he was bluffing."

"So, solve this for me, will you?"

"Don't you want to Xerox it first and give me a copy?"

"No need. It's not evidence. There isn't a crime scene. There's no crime. It's just a crossword puzzle."

"That's the problem, Chief. Under those circumstances I can't work up any enthusiasm for it."

"I'm not asking you to blurb it. I'm just asking you to solve it."

"Blurb it?"

"Isn't that what writers call it when they praise each other's work?"

"How should I know?"

"Aren't you a writer?"

"In the loosest sense," Cora said truthfully. She hated to lie. If necessary, she did so with a straight face, but she much preferred to concoct an absolute truth that totally misled the person asking. Calling herself a writer in the loosest sense of the word certainly filled the bill. The sense could not be looser.

Harper was not easily deflected. "Be that as it may. I would like to know what his puzzle says. Mainly so I can cross it off my list of things to do."

"You have a long list, Chief?"

"Is that nice? Business is admittedly slow. Early this morning I was thinking of setting a speed trap."

"No one speeds around here."

"Almost no one. Good thing I didn't look at the speedometer when I was chasing you."

"Is that a threat, Chief? Solve this for me and I won't run you in for speeding?"

Harper was shocked. "Of course not." He shrugged. "Though it's a wonderful idea. So, what do you say?"

"How soon do you need it?"

"I'd like it tonight. You could fax me the answer."

"I'm not good with the fax machine."

"So read it over the phone."

"The whole puzzle?"

"No, just the theme answer. That's all that really matters, right?"

"How the hell should I know? I didn't write the damn thing."

"You're a little touchy, Cora."

"I'm disappointed. You come to me with a dead man and a puzzle. You insist it means nothing, but you torture me with it anyway. It's cruel and unusual punishment. It ought to be illegal. No taunting the Puzzle Lady."

"Very funny. Just have it by tonight."

Cora couldn't believe how quickly it had all gone wrong. Here she was, minding her own business. Well, other people's business, actually, but she was minding it. Honing her detective skills by following random people to the mall. How could she possibly get in trouble doing that?

Only she had.

And now she was faced with having to solve a crossword puzzle.

How could she get out of it?

Cora smiled.

Of course.
Harvey Beerbaum.

CHAPTER 4

Harvey Beerbaum was beaming all over his face. "I can't begin to thank you."

"You've already begun, Harvey," Cora said. The little cruciverbalist had ambushed Cora in Cushman's Bake Shop, seemed determined to ruin her latte and scone.

"Yes, but to the chief of police. Who always asks you first. Of course, he's known you longer, but still. To recommend me."

"You're an expert, Harvey. Why wouldn't I recommend you?"

"Because you always do it yourself. That's how it works. Chief Harper comes to you. You give him the answer. I read about it in the paper." Harvey realized he had taken on a petulant tone. "Not that I'm complaining," he said to apologize for complaining. "It's just that's what you do. Except in this case you recommended me."

"I'm going to take my coffee outside, Harvey. It's a lovely day. I'd like to sit on the

30

bench. Unless there's someone there." Cora looked through the front window. "No. There isn't. I'm going to sit out there."

She made good her escape.

Harvey, who hadn't ordered yet, stayed inside.

Cora sat on the bench, sipped her latte, nibbled her scone. Hoped someone else would sit on the bench before Harvey came out.

No one did. The portly puzzle maker came dancing out the door on little cat feet, pirouetted to the bench. Were it not for his awkward, embarrassed advances, Cora would have thought he was gay.

"So," Harvey said. "Here you sit alone. Such an attractive woman shouldn't have to sit alone."

"Yeah, I was unlucky," Cora said.

Harvey raised his eyebrows. "Excuse me?"

"Sit down, Harvey. You make me nervous hovering."

"Yes, of course." Harvey plopped himself down, put his muffin on the bench between them, sipped his coffee. "I just want to thank you for sending Chief Harper to me."

"You've done that, Harvey. Several times."

"I know. It's just so unlike you. To share the limelight." His eyes widened, and he blushed splendidly. "I didn't mean that the

31

way it sounded. It sounded terrible. That's not what I meant at all."

"Relax, Harvey. I'm not offended. That's not to say you're not offensive. You just don't bother me."

Harvey plowed right through the barb as if he hadn't heard it. That was the first hint Cora had she might be in trouble.

"I solved the puzzle for Chief Harper, and I brought you a copy in case you wanted to see it. I figured you'd want to see it, even if you didn't care enough to solve it. Do you want to see it?"

"Well, if you brought it along."

Harvey didn't produce the puzzle. Instead, he took a sip of his coffee. "I had a feeling you did. So I started to put two and two together. What do you think I found?"

"Would the answer be four?"

"Your niece is on her honeymoon, isn't she?"

Uh-oh.

Yes," Cora said. "She and Aaron went to Africa."

"So if you had to solve a puzzle, you couldn't count on her for help."

"What's your point?"

"So, instead, you passed the puzzle on to me. This confirms something I have long suspected."

Oh, hell. Of all the people in the world Cora didn't want to learn her secret, Harvey Beerbaum was near the top of the list. Fussy, pedantic, gossipy, and a stickler for the rules, Harvey wouldn't hesitate to blow her cover. Only the threat of being sued for slander might stop him. That or blackmail. Did the man have secret vices? A collection of erotic pottery, perchance? If so, could Cora uncover it in time to do her any good?

"Harvey, you've been reading too many murder mysteries," Cora said. "Coming up with intrigues and plot twists and bizarre double crosses."

Harvey shook his head. "No, no. You're not going to put me off this time." He leaned in confidentially. "I know your secret, Puzzle Lady."

Cora felt sick. "Oh, you do, do you?"

"Yes, I do. This proves it."

"Proves what?"

He cocked his head, raised a knowing eyebrow. "You're a constructor."

Cora blinked. "What?"

Harvey nodded emphatically. "A constructor. Not a solver. You can only construct. Not solve. If you're asked to solve a puzzle that's not your own, you haven't a clue how to go about it."

"Oh."

"Which explains why you never solve a puzzle on the spot, you always take it home and bring it back. It took a while for me to notice, but I finally caught on."

"I see."

"You can't deny it. It's as plain as the nose on your face." Harvey's mouth fell open. "I didn't mean to say that, either. Your nose isn't plain. Quite the contrary. It's a very nice nose. A handsome nose. I mean a pretty nose. Oh, for goodness' sakes, I don't know what I mean."

"Eat your muffin, Harvey, before you have a nervous breakdown."

Harvey subsided, nibbled his muffin. Cora nibbled her scone.

"Okay, Harvey, you got me. I'm not as quick as you are at solving puzzles. Crossword puzzles, anyway. I can take you at sudoku. But I'm not a swift solver. I've never entered the national tournament, and I never will. If you want to humiliate me, there's nothing I can do."

Harvey looked shocked. "I would never dream of such a thing."

"Then what's your point?"

"No point. Just that I was right."

Cora patted him on the cheek. "Harvey, Harvey, of course you're right. You're a constructor *and* a solver. I'm not. I'm better at solving mysteries. Like this dead guy. Who killed him? That's what I want to know."

Harvey looked at her in alarm. "Someone killed him?"

"Isn't that what the puzzle says?"

"Not at all."

"Well, that's disappointing. I was hoping you'd bring me news of a murder. 'Check my son-in-law's suitcase for poison,' or something like that."

"I assure you I'd have mentioned a murder weapon."

"That's better, Harvey. You're back to your old, feisty self. Well, what about it? What's the theme entry? Did he embed a poem?"

"He sure did. Take a look."

Cora took the puzzle, read, " 'At noon I can not be done. So I should try to at one.' What the hell does *that* mean?"

"I was hoping you could tell me."

"Well, I haven't a clue. What does Chief Harper think?"

"He's glad it doesn't mean anything. He was afraid there'd be something he'd have to investigate."

"This poem doesn't fill the bill. It's meaningless."

"Unless something else comes up."

"Like what?"

"I have no idea."

Cora finished her latte, tossed the paper cup in the trash can at the end of the bench, and handed the crossword back to Harvey.

"Oh, keep it," he said. "I have my own copy. That's for you."

Cora plunged the crossword into her floppy drawstring purse, wondered if Harvey'd go away if she lit a cigarette. She had been trying to quit, partly at Sherry's urging that it hurt her image but also from a recent shortness of breath, which did *not* indicate she was getting old.

Cora heaved herself up from the bench, nodded at Harvey, who still had some muffin left, and walked off.

Her car was parked opposite the police station. She considered dropping in on Chief Harper to see what he really thought of the puzzle. She immediately shelved the idea. That would make him think she was giving it credence. Which she certainly wasn't. She just wished she were.

Cora climbed into the Toyota, backed out of the parking space. She felt good driving home. She'd averted the Harvey Beerbaum disaster. Not being quick at solving puzzles was a secret she was happy to share. It was a far cry from confessing to not really being the Puzzle Lady. She'd dodged that bullet. And she'd dodged a bullet when Harper gave her the puzzle in the first place. She'd done it without panicking and calling Sherry in Kenya. She'd done it all on her own. Sherry was having a honeymoon, and Cora was coping. That was how it should be, and that was how it was. Business as usual.

Cora pulled into the driveway of the modest ranch house she shared with Sherry and Aaron. She went up the front path, opened the door. Buddy shot out, raced around the yard in crazy circles, as if trying to make up in speed what he lacked in stature.

Cora followed the toy poodle back inside, where the answering machine was beeping. She hoped it was a bridge game. Cora liked bridge games. They played for money.

Beep.

"This is Betty Rosenberg at the Associated Press. Our fax line is down. Could you please e-mail the Puzzle Lady column as an attached file?"

Cora groaned. Boy, talk about a mood killer. She had never attached a file in her life, let alone sent one. How could she possibly do that? Screwed, blued, and tattooed.

She'd have to call Sherry in Africa after all. What the hell time was it in Kenya? What was Sherry's phone number? Cora'd paid no attention because she wasn't going to use it, and now, here she was in a mess where she had no choice, and she didn't know how to do it. Why hadn't she listened? What a moron — she'd brought this all on herself.

Wait a minute. She had Sherry's phone number. It was written down in the office. That was what Sherry said. Written down in the office. On the same page as the instructions for faxing the puzzles. Emergency numbers.

Cora hurried into the office.

Yes, of course. It was right there.

Along with . . .

On page two of the instructions was the heading ATTACHED FILE SENDING FOR DUMMIES.

Cora wasn't offended. She was never so relieved in her life. She clicked on the mouse, opened her e-mail.

The computer crashed.

CHAPTER 5

The science teacher was offended. "A what?"

"A computer nerd. I need a computer nerd."

"We don't call them computer nerds."

"What do you call them?"

"We call them technical assistants."

"Okay, I need a technical assistant."

"Why?"

"My computer crashed."

"How did it crash?"

"How? Well, it's not like I dropped it on the floor."

"What does it look like?"

"Well, the screen turned blue."

"Ah! The blue screen of death!"

"You know what it is?"

"Yes."

"Can you fix it?"

"That's not so easy."

"That's why I need a computer nerd."

"A technical assistant."

"Yes."

"I'll send one over."

The science teacher sent over a technician, who differed from a computer nerd in his title. He had dark-rimmed glasses, a big nose, and pencils and pens in a pocket protector.

Cora wondered if she should really be blamed for perpetuating the stereotype.

Whatever you called him, the guy was good. Within twenty minutes, he had rebooted the computer and discovered the source of the problem, which Cora still didn't understand in spite of his explaining it to her in computerese so condescending he was lucky she didn't rap him upside the head.

"It's very simple," he said in a nasal whine that set her teeth on edge. "If you don't power down correctly, and you leave your virus protection off . . ." He shook a gloomy head. "How many windows did you have open when you crashed?"

"Windows?"

"Programs. Crossword Compiler, for instance. Did you have Crossword Compiler open?"

"No," Cora said with absolute assurance. Nothing could have induced her to open a

41

crossword-puzzle-constructing program.

"How about eBay, Amazon.com, *Days of Our Lives* official Web site, iTunes, International Movie Database, Fandango, and Date Match?"

"Well, if you're going to count every little thing."

"You can't leave all your programs open. It's like leaving your doors open. What happens when you leave your doors open?"

"My computer gets stolen?" Cora said hopefully.

"No, you get the blue screen of death."

"And that's not good?"

He gave her a baleful look. "It's not funny. You think it's just you, but it's not. You're on the Web. When you e-mail a friend, you're not just touching their computer, you're touching every computer they've ever touched."

"I'll wear a condom," Cora said. The young man looked shocked. "I get it. I've been a bad girl. Can I use the computer now?"

"Of course you can. But it's going to crash again if you're not careful. I can't keep running over here."

"You've only run over here once. I don't think that's enough to claim a pattern."

"Remember what I told you?"

"You told me a lot of things."

"When your computer freezes. Remember what to do then?"

"I'm guessing it has nothing to do with hot chocolate."

"Remember what three keys you hit?"

"Control, Alt, Delete."

"You *were* paying attention."

"Well, it reminded me of my fifth husband."

"What?"

"The acronym. CAD."

"Oh."

"So that will unfreeze my computer?"

"No. It will let you turn it off."

"What do you mean, *let* me turn it off? I can *always* turn it off."

"No, you can't."

"Sure I can. I can pull the plug."

"Yeah. If you want to risk damaging your computer and losing data."

"That's the only downside?"

"And you get the blue screen of death."

"I hate it when that happens."

"Turn it off the way I taught you, and you should be able to reboot."

"And I do that by . . . ?"

"Turning it on again."

"Let me be sure I got this straight. The entire wit and wisdom of your approach to computer dynamics is turn it off and turn it back on?"

"If you want to think of it that way."

"You want me to try it to show I can do it?"

"That won't be necessary. It's working now. But if it gets frozen again, you know what to do." He got up from the desk chair. "Say, where'd you get the computer puzzle?"

"What computer puzzle?"

Cora had taken the crossword puzzle Harvey had given her out of her purse. It was lying on the desk.

"That's not a computer puzzle. It's done in pen and ink."

"Yeah, but it's all about computers."

"What do you mean, it's all about computers?"

"Well, take a look." He pointed. "Right across the bottom you've got *screen, net, disk, mouse.* They're all computer terms. Whoever constructed this puzzle went to a lot of trouble to call attention to computers."

Cora frowned.

"Is that right?"

CHAPTER 6

Dr. Barney Nathan looked dapper as ever in a bright red bow tie. His manner, however, was somewhat less than cordial. "I don't know why you expect me to help you."

"Don't be silly. You're a doctor."

"You said I was a bad doctor."

"No, I didn't." Cora shrugged. "I may have said you botched a few autopsies."

"That's the same thing."

"No, it isn't. Bad doctors kill people. I assume the ones you autopsy are already dead."

"That's not funny. You said those things in public."

"I did?"

"You know you did. You said it to Chief Harper. You said it in the town meeting. You said it on TV."

"Yes, but it isn't true."

"That's slander."

"So what? Truth is defense for slander."

"What?"

"You didn't do it, so you can't be slandered."

"That's *not* what it means," Barney cried indignantly. "Just the opposite. If something is true, it isn't slander."

"Well, isn't it true you didn't botch the autopsy? You didn't botch it, did you, Barney?"

"You *know* I didn't botch the autopsy."

"Then what are we arguing about?"

Barney Nathan sputtered to a standstill, his mind short-circuited by Cora's breezy doublespeak.

"And here's your chance to prove it," Cora said. "With your autopsy on Mr. Overmeyer."

"I didn't perform an autopsy on Mr. Overmeyer."

"Why not?"

"He died of natural causes."

"How do you know?"

"It's on the death certificate."

"Who signed the death certificate?"

"I did."

Cora nodded. "I see. Then you examined the body?"

"I examined it for signs of life. There were none. I pronounced him dead."

"From what cause?"

"Old age."

"That's a disease?"

"Of course not."

"Then what did he die of?"

"Organ failure."

"Which one?"

"All of them."

"What does it say on the death certificate?"

"I don't remember."

"Could you look?"

"There's no reason to."

"You'd do it for Chief Harper."

"You're not him."

"No, but if I ask him, he'll ask you. Why don't we cut out the middleman?"

Grumbling to himself, Barney Nathan rifled through his files, pulled out a chart. "He died of renal failure. As a result of cancer."

"Really?"

"Yes, really."

"No sign of foul play?"

"Of course not."

"Why do you say that?"

"He's an old man. He had no money."

"Those are medical reasons?"

"Those are commonsense reasons. Come on, Cora. I'd be more sympathetic if you hadn't ripped me in public."

"Where is the gentleman?"

"At the hospital morgue."

"Really? I thought it was a natural death. Why isn't he at the funeral home?"

"Kelly likes to be paid. Funny that way."

"You're telling me Mr. Overmeyer has no relatives and no cash?"

"That's how I understand it."

"That's really the reason, isn't it? The guy's being passed over because he has no relatives and no cash."

"That's not true."

"Then you'll look at the body?"

"No."

"You'll let me look at the body?"

"No."

"That's rather petty, Barney."

"I don't care. The fact is, there's no reason under the sun for me to look at the body."

"Suppose I gave you one."

"What?"

"He left a crossword puzzle."

"Indicating he'd been killed?"

"No."

"Indicating foul play?"

"No."

"Indicating he had money hidden somewhere we didn't know about?"

"No. Nothing like that."

"Indicating what?"

"I have no idea."

"Of course not. But since puzzles are your specialty, you'd like to assume it has some importance, and pass that on to me. So, unless you'd like to show me that puzzle and point out the reasons it shows an autopsy is indicated . . ."

"Come on, Barney. Do me a favor."

"Why in the world should I do you a favor?"

"Well, for one thing, I'm here talking to you instead of talking to Rick Reed."

The doctor's eyes widened at the mention of the Channel Eight news reporter. "Are you threatening me? If I don't give you what you want, you'll take it on TV?"

"Certainly not, Barney." Cora smiled. "But thanks for the suggestion."

CHAPTER 7

Cora Felton was on the computer playing FreeCell, instant-messaging with a man she'd met in a chat room, and bidding on a mink stole on eBay when Buddy raced into the office, barking furiously. Cora couldn't hear the toy poodle because she was listening to music on iTunes, but she caught sight of him, sprang from her chair, and nearly strangled herself with her headset. She ripped it off and leapt to close the computer screen. She wasn't sure which embarrassed her more, the man or the mink. It would be just her luck to buy it and have some animal rights activist splash her with red paint.

But it wasn't an unannounced visitor. Just an insistently ringing phone. Cora scooped it up.

It was Chief Harper. "So you *are* there. How come you don't answer? I've been ringing and ringing."

"I didn't hear it. I was listening to music."

50

"So loud you couldn't hear the phone?"

"Pink Floyd, Chief. You gotta play it loud. So, what's up?"

"You went to Barney Nathan. Browbeat him into doing an autopsy."

"Oh."

"Which wouldn't be so bad if you hadn't implied I sanctioned your actions."

"I don't think I did that."

"Did you tell Barney if he didn't do it, you'd ask me to ask him?"

"Oh, that."

"Did you threaten him with TV exposure?"

"So, Barney ratted me out. I didn't think he would."

"He didn't rat you out."

"No?"

"I asked probing questions. He had no recourse but to reply."

" 'No recourse' sounds very official, police-mattery, Chief. You really mean to say that?"

"There's a lot of ways to get Barney to do an autopsy. Threatening him with the media and pretending I asked for it shouldn't make the short list."

"I'm a bad girl. You can tell Barney you bawled me out."

"No, I can't."

"Why not?"

"Barney found a whacking dose of arsenic inside the corpse."

"Oops."

"That is a *wonderful* assessment of the situation."

"Well, what do you want me to say? We were looking for foul play. We found foul play. What's wrong with that?"

"*You* were looking for foul play. *I* wasn't."

"So what, Chief? You think I'm going to go running around saying you overlooked it?"

"No. Can you speak for Barney Nathan?"

"Sure. He's not going to go running around telling people *he* overlooked it. What's he doing with the news?"

"I told him to sit on it."

"Good move. You can release a statement how he autopsied the body on your suggestion."

"And why did I ask for the autopsy?"

"The crossword puzzle made you suspicious."

"Which leads me right back to you."

"No," Cora said triumphantly. "Which leads you right back to Harvey Beerbaum."

There was silence on the line while Harper mulled that over.

"So, the guy was murdered," Cora said.

"Why would anybody do that?"

"Why indeed. There was no money in-volved."

"And no relatives?"

"Not so far. I'm trying to track down a great-nephew. He seems to have outlived everyone else."

"How about friends?"

"So far no one has stepped up."

"I'd sure like to see the crime scene."

"What crime scene?"

"His house."

"That's not a crime scene."

"It is now."

CHAPTER 8

The late Mr. Overmeyer lived in a rickety cabin just far enough outside of town to have escaped stricter zoning laws, which might have required such things as a patched roof, a coat of paint, or at least two hinges on the screen door, as Cora discovered when it nearly took off her arm.

"On second thought, Chief, you go first."

Chief Harper, strolling laconically up the walk, produced a set of keys from his pocket. "That was always my intention."

He unlocked the front door, pushed it open.

The smell that assaulted them was truly overpowering.

"The corpse is gone?" Cora said.

"I'm quite sure."

"Could there be another one?"

"I'd prefer there wasn't."

"Killjoy."

Chief Harper switched on the light.

The place was filthy. The floor was littered with dust, old newspapers, pinecones, tin cans, beer bottles, a Domino's Pizza box, and a pair of boots. A half-eaten apple lay in the corner. Ants crawled over it.

"I think I saw this house on *Curb Appeal*," Cora said.

"Aw, it's nothing a carpenter, a plumber, and an exterminator couldn't fix."

"And perhaps a demolitions expert."

"What are we looking for here?"

Cora shrugged. "Don't ask me. You're the big-time police chief. I'm just along for the ride."

"As if."

"Okay, where was the body?"

"Why would I see the body? An old man dies of natural causes. Happens all the time. You think I see them all?"

"You're saying you *didn't* see the body?"

Harper sighed. "You should have been a lawyer. Yeah, I saw the body. Not because Barney suspected foul play. Because of the damn crossword."

"What did you think the puzzle meant?"

"Nothing. Absolutely nothing."

"Then why did you ask me to solve it?"

"That's what you do with crossword puzzles. You solve them."

"Uh-huh. So where was the corpse?"

"Right there on the couch."

"Sitting up?"

"Sort of keeled over."

"So. He was sitting on the couch, decided he didn't want to go on living, and just flopped down."

"The arsenic might have had a hand in that decision."

"Granted. I notice there is no glass or other beaker on the coffee table that might have contained poison."

"No, there isn't."

"Was there when you saw the body?"

Harper said nothing. Cora looked at him. He appeared red in the face.

"Oh."

"There was no reason to suspect foul play."

"Of course not."

"But *you* did. Which is somewhat embarrassing to a man in my position. So, if you have some wacky idea about all this, I would be grateful if you'd share the information."

"I don't know anything you don't know."

"You just interpreted it better."

"Did I say that?"

"No. You just deduced it was a murder, and demanded an autopsy."

"That was largely wishful thinking, Chief."

"Come on, Cora. What tipped you off?"

"Need you ask?"

Chief Harper's eyes widened. "Are you saying it was the crossword puzzle?"

"I'm not saying that. I'm specifically *not* saying it was the crossword puzzle."

"But it was."

"Why do you say that, Chief? I'd love to hear your theory."

"Harvey solved the crossword puzzle. It was meaningless drivel. 'At noon I can not be done. So I should try to at one.' That's less than helpful." He cocked his head. "Unless you know better."

"Absolutely not, Chief. I find it just as unhelpful as you do."

"So, what's with the puzzle? Come on. Give."

Cora pulled the puzzle out of her purse, showed the references to Chief Harper.

"A computer?"

"Yes."

"It's a puzzle about a computer?"

"I wouldn't go that far. But there's enough references to make it possible."

"And Harvey missed it."

"Don't blame Harvey, Chief. He solved the puzzle."

"Are you saying he missed it because he solved the puzzle?"

"I'm just saying since he was bent on solving the puzzle, it's not surprising his attention was elsewhere."

"Are you saying you noticed because you *didn't* solve the puzzle?"

"I'm not saying that either."

"You're just saying it was easier."

"You're putting words in my mouth, Chief."

"I bet if you solved the puzzle, you'd have noticed. I know you. There's no way that you could solve that puzzle and not notice."

"I suppose that's partly true," Cora said. She didn't point out the part that was true was that there was no way she could solve the puzzle. She felt a little guilty about taking credit for the computer nerd's findings, but as long as Sherry was out of the country, she needed to take credit for something.

Chief Harper exhaled, glanced around the filthy kitchen. "So. We're looking for a computer."

"You're not happy with that theory, Chief."

"Do you think this guy had a computer?"

"More likely an abacus."

Chief Harper pulled open a wooden door. "What's that?" Cora said. "The pantry?"

"The cellar."

"This place has a cellar?"

"More like a crawl space. Wanna come down?"

"Is there a light?"

"I got a flashlight."

"Good for you. What's down there?"

"Rats. Spiders."

"You don't really see that. You're just trying to keep me out."

Cora peered over Chief Harper's shoulder. His flashlight lit up three wooden steps down to a dirt floor. The rats were an invention. But from the cobwebs, she had a feeling the spiders were real.

"I bow to your expertise, Chief. You check out the cellar."

Harper disappeared down the stairs. "Aha!"

"What's that?"

"Well, we got half a ten-speed bicycle."

"You mean a five-speed bicycle?"

"Ha ha. The water pipes and electrical cables have been here since the dawn of time. The heating duct looks newer, probably installed in response to some building code violation. . . . Yup. It's dated 2003 with a serial number. I get the impression the only time Overmeyer repaired the cabin was under threat of being shut down."

"You see anything looks like a computer?"

"Very funny."

"It's not funny. It's the thing we're looking for. How about high-speed Internet
cable? Any cable running under there?"

"There's a phone line."

"Does it look like it was installed before
there was Internet?"

"It looks like it was installed before there
were phones."

Chief Harper came out of the stairwell.
His face was covered with cobwebs and dirt.

"You got a dinner engagement tonight,
Chief?"

"Why?"

"No reason."

Harper went into the kitchen and washed
his face. There was no towel. He dried it on
his sleeve.

A wooden stairway led to the second floor.
The cabin, though small, had dormers,
creating an upstairs bedroom. There was a
brass bed, minus the headboard. On the
wall behind it hung a framed picture of
poker-playing dogs.

A wooden dresser with crooked drawers
did not hold a computer. Cora sorted
through tattered boxer shorts, wool socks
with holes in the heels, plaid flannel shirts,
white undershirts, faded khaki pants.

"Anything in the closet?" she asked.

"Couple of sweaters. A sweatshirt. Tweed

sports jacket looks like it's never been worn."

"Anything in the pockets?"

"No. Or in the lining, if that's your next question. I patted it down."

Cora came over. "What else we got?"

"Some shoes. Some men's magazines. A box of junk."

"What do you mean, junk?"

Harper pulled back the top of the cardboard box. There was no computer. Not even a pocket calculator. A couple of books without covers. A busted lamp. An ashtray. Some coat hangers. Some light bulbs. Some scattered playing cards, not nearly a full deck. A Monopoly game, box ripped, properties falling out. "See? Junk."

"In other words, there's no reason in the world for keeping that box," Cora said.

"That's right."

"Move it."

"Huh?"

"Pull it out of the closet so I can see."

Chief Harper wrestled the box out into the room. To his annoyance, Cora ignored it completely. She went into the closet, examined the floor.

"Here, Chief. Those floorboards look loose to you?"

The floorboards *were* loose. Chief Harper

pried them up.

There was a space below the floor. He reached in, pulled out a gun.

CHAPTER 9

Cora was offended. "I don't see why you're upset with me."

"Oh, you don't?" Chief Harper settled back in his desk chair, tapped a pencil into his hand. "Let's find a reason. You suspect a murder, demand an autopsy, which produces poison. You send me out to the quote scene of the crime unquote, in the guise of looking for a computer, and within minutes direct me to the hiding place of a gun."

"I don't think that's a fair assessment of the facts."

"Where am I wrong?"

Cora reached into her floppy drawstring purse, pulled out her cigarettes.

"You can't smoke."

"That's not fair."

"Yes, it is. You finesse me into letting you smoke when I want your help. This is a slightly different situation. You've been brought in for questioning."

"That's a little unfair, Chief. We're having a nice conversation here. No one's charging anyone with anything. No one's advising anyone of their rights."

"You're sparring, Cora."

"I'm doing nothing of the sort. You just think I am because you've got this notion in your head that I set this all in motion because I knew about the gun."

"Are you claiming you didn't?"

"Of course I didn't."

"You didn't go to the crime scene, search around, find a gun, leave it where it was, and go suggest Barney autopsy the body?"

"No, I didn't."

"And you didn't find it there *after* he autopsied the body, leave it there, go and get me, and suggest we search the place?"

"That's partly true, Chief."

"Oh?"

"I suggested we search the place. That's true. It's the bit about finding the gun that isn't."

"You just walked into the cabin and within minutes found the guy's hiding place?"

"It was the logical place to look."

"Under a box of junk?"

"Yes."

"Why?"

"The junk had no reason being in that

closet *except* to hide something under it."

"That's a fine explanation. I'm not sure I believe it, but I certainly admire it."

"So, what's the scoop on the gun, Chief? Since I found it, it's only fair I know."

"I'm assuming you know already."

"What? It's a thirty-two-caliber Smith and Wesson revolver with one empty shell in the cylinder, and it hasn't been fired recently. Aside from that, I haven't a clue."

Chief Harper looked at her narrowly. "And how do you know that?"

"Give me a break, Chief. I was there when you found it." Cora reached in her drawstring purse, pulled out a gun. "It's a Smith and Wesson, just like this. Except smaller. Mine's a thirty-eight, so it's a thirty-two. If it had been fired recently, you'd have known it, but you didn't, so it hadn't. As for the empty shell in the cylinder, that's a guess. But if there wasn't, you wouldn't be taking all this interest."

"How'd you know it was only one?"

"I didn't. I figured if it was more than one, you'd tell me."

"There were two."

"Really? That's interesting."

Harper frowned. "You make it sound so logical."

"You think it's more logical I killed someone with Overmeyer's gun, then slipped him a whacking dose of poison to cover up the fact I'd done it?"

"You think someone did that?"

Cora shrugged. "It's as good a guess as any. So, you tracing the gun?"

"Dan's running it now. He should have something soon."

There was a knock on the door.

"Well, that's timing."

"Yeah," Cora said. "A movie moment."

Dan Finley poked his head in the door. The young officer was a Puzzle Lady fan. "Hi, Cora. You under arrest?"

"Not yet. He's working on it."

"You trace the serial number on that gun?" Harper asked him.

Dan shook his head. "It's old. Before they had computers. It's going to take some time. Anyway, Becky Baldwin's here to see you."

Harper frowned. "Why?"

Dan shrugged. "She's a lawyer. She must have a reason."

"You didn't ask."

"I was distracted. I'm trying to trace a gun."

"Send her in."

"With Cora here?"

"Why not. Be interesting to see if she

objects. Send her in."

Becky Baldwin was probably not everyone's idea of a lawyer. Too young, too blond, too thin, too stylish, too attractive, she looked more like a supermodel than an attorney.

Becky took in Cora with a glance, said, "You want her here?"

Harper shrugged. "It's your show. Do *you* want her here?"

"Doesn't matter."

"Now there's a compliment," Cora observed. "Mind if I quote that on my résumé? 'Doesn't matter.' "

"I have a legal problem," Becky said.

"Well, you've come to the right place," Cora told her. "He's a cop. You're a lawyer. What could be better?"

"Maybe you *should* wait outside," Becky said.

Cora pantomimed zipping her lip. "No, no. I'll be good."

"What do you want?" Harper said. "I hate to hurry you, but I have this homicide."

"Really? I hadn't heard."

"It hasn't been released yet. Old Mr. Overmeyer died. Turns out it was murder."

"Well, if you arrest anyone for it, could you give 'em my card?"

"That would be illegal."

"Relax," Cora said. "You're the only lawyer in town."

"Are you working on this?" Becky asked.

"At the moment I'm a suspect. If he arrests me, I'll give you a call. Somehow I doubt that's going to happen."

"If you uncover the murderer . . ."

"I'll be sure to recommend you," Cora said.

"What do you need?" Harper prompted.

"Oh. Well, Sherry and Aaron finally got married and went on their honeymoon."

Cora nodded. "Tough break. But it was bound to happen. I wouldn't worry about it, though. There's a lot of opportunities out there for a girl like you."

Becky's eyes widened, then blazed. "I didn't say I was jealous. I said it's a problem."

"Why?"

"Sherry being out of town is a problem. I'm the attorney of record for Dennis Pride. There is, as you know, a restraining order keeping him away from his ex-wife. Which is just fine as long as she's here."

Cora's eyes widened. "You mean . . . ?"

"With her gone it's moot."

"Dennis has been around?"

"All the time. Ever since she left. Haven't you seen him?"

"I haven't been looking for him."

"Who has? He drops in to see me on the pretext of discussing his probation. Not that there's anything to discuss. He's got two more years running on his suspended sentence. I can't wait till it's over."

"He'll just hire you again," Cora said.

"For what?"

"Anything he can think of. Hell, I wouldn't put it past him to kill someone just so he needs representation."

"Fine. I can use the work. The point is, he's here, he's going to get in trouble, and I've got no legal reason to force him to leave."

"What do you expect me to do about it?" Chief Harper said.

"Couldn't you bring him in, have a little talk with him, suggest he's not doing himself any good?"

"You mean hassle him for no earthly reason?"

"That's not the way I would have put it."

"Really, Becky. There's nothing I can do."

"How about you, Cora?"

"Me? That's a good one. You're asking me to harass your client?"

"Again, that's not the precise terminology I had in mind."

"Gee, Chief," Cora said. "You've got a

murder investigation. Couldn't you pick him up for questioning?"

"On what grounds?"

"I don't know. You say he's been hanging around since Sherry left. Was he here when the murder happened?"

"When did it happen?" Becky asked.

"Well, let's see," Cora said. "You brought me the puzzle —"

"Puzzle?" Becky said.

"Oh, hell."

"What's this about a puzzle?"

"There was a puzzle by Overmeyer's body. It turns out it doesn't mean anything. But it made me hassle Barney, and he found arsenic."

"Overmeyer was killed how long ago, Chief?"

"Two nights ago. But that's not the point. The point is, nobody knows it yet. So don't tell anyone."

Becky smiled.

"Of course not."

CHAPTER 10

Rick Reed, Channel Eight's clueless on-camera reporter, was puffed up with his own importance. "Murder in Bakerhaven," he declared. "In a Channel Eight exclusive, the death of Mr. Herbert Overmeyer, originally believed to be of natural causes, has been deemed suspicious by the medical examiner, and will be announced tomorrow as a homicide. The chief of police could not be reached for comment —" Rick raised an eyebrow insinuatingly at the implications of that — "but I am coming to you live from Bakerhaven with an exclusive interview with Bakerhaven attorney Rebecca Baldwin."

The camera pulled back to include Becky, looking like a high-priced law firm's brightest new junior partner in a stylish yet no-nonsense purple pantsuit.

Rick was pleased as punch to have her. "I am standing here in front of the Bakerhaven Police Station, where to date there have been no arrests in the murder of Mr. Over-meyer. That's right, I said murder. Ms. Baldwin, what can you tell us about this affair?"

"Absolutely nothing, Rick."

Rick Reed's face fell. "That was my understanding."

Becky smiled. "I am an attorney-at-law. At the moment, I am not representing a client. I would only be able to comment in the event that the police make an arrest, and that the arrested person contacts me."

"You mean the killer?"

"Certainly not. I mean the accused. Anyone can be falsely accused and need representation. In which case I am sure I'd have a lot to say."

"Isn't it true the Overmeyer case is about to be announced as a homicide?"

"That's hearsay, Rick. I'm not in a position to confirm it."

"But is it not a fact that Dr. Barney Nathan conducted an autopsy on the body and discovered arsenic?"

"I'm not in a position to confirm that, either."

"But wouldn't that make it a homicide?"

"I would think so. Unless the arsenic was taken accidentally. Or voluntarily."

"Are you aware that Chief Harper had no

comment on the situation?"

"Chief Harper said no comment?"

"Chief Harper could not be reached for comment."

"If you do reach him, could you find out who he suspects?"

"I certainly will. This is Rick Reed, Channel Eight News."

The news crew lowered the camera.

Rick looked peeved. "I thought you were going to confirm the murder."

Becky smiled. "You know I can't do that."

"You told me it was."

"Yeah. So?"

"Why didn't you say so?"

"I can't say something on TV if I can't prove it. You know that."

Rick looked like a little boy the smarty-pants girl on the playground tricked out of his milk money. "You said you'd give me an exclusive if I'd buy you lunch."

"Are you trying to get out of buying me lunch?"

"No, but —"

"Because I don't recall promising to say anything in particular."

"But I went on TV and said I had a homicide."

"Relax. You do."

"Can you confirm that?"

"Only by hearsay."

"We're not in court. Can you positively confirm the Overmeyer case is a homicide?"

"Absolutely."

Rick thought that over.

"Then lunch is on Channel Eight."

CHAPTER 11

Cora hated takeout. At least in Bakerhaven. In Manhattan, takeout was a joy. At a mere touch of a button, she could have Thai, Japanese, Indian, French, Italian, Mexican, or Cuban arrive at her doorstep. Bakerhaven takeout consisted of mediocre Chinese you had to pick up yourself or the wedges of congealed sauce and cheese that had presumably been pizza before the pimply-faced high school boy bicycled great distances to deliver it stone cold.

There was a Burger King in the mall, but it wasn't a real Burger King with a handy drive-up window where one could score a Whopper anonymously without comment, merely an adjunct of the food court outside the Cineplex, where one couldn't help but feel self-conscious standing in line amid a gaggle of giggling teenage girls.

For a woman of Cora's culinary talents (none), this presented quite a problem.

The solution was to go out to dinner. But Cora couldn't stand dining alone. It made her feel like a lonely old spinster. She had no potential husband in tow. Her only current suitor was Harvey Beerbaum, whom she rated just ahead of the Ebola virus. She could always dine with the girls on bridge night, but that was only once a week, and what should she do with the other six?

Tonight, Cora had put off the decision forever, vacillating from one unappetizing choice to another, until by ten o'clock, ravenous, stomach growling, she had hopped in the Toyota and sped off to Starbucks for a venti Frappuccino, that scrumptious, life-affirming calorie fest, a guilty pleasure worth every wiggle it took to squirm inside her slinky party dress; after all, who was she trying to impress, anyway?

Starbucks was closed, saving her from herself.

If Cora was grateful, she did not show it. They were lucky she didn't lob a brick through the window.

She went home, rooted through the refrigerator for some tidbits she might have overlooked. There were none. In the cupboard she found a box of cornflakes. On inspection, they were not Granville Grains, the company she hawked on TV. It didn't matter. Cora hated cold cereal. Even so, she was past the point of being picky. If she had to eat cereal, she could eat cereal.

Provided she had milk.

She did. It smelled a little rank. She checked the date: only six days beyond expiration. Surely milk ought to hold up better than that.

Cora put the carton back in the refrigerator. It didn't occur to her to throw it out. Not that she might be desperate enough to try it later, but disposing of rancid milk was beyond her expertise.

She found a bag of egg noodles. That was promising. Cora could recall eating egg noodles. Some of Sherry's more delicious concoctions had included them. And Cora knew how to make noodles. You boiled water, put in the noodles. Wasn't that right? Cora checked the package. It was. Of course, they said something about how many quarts of water, and adding salt, and stirring, and how many minutes, but that seemed overly technical.

Cora filled a saucepan with water, lit a burner, turned it on to high.

Waited for it to boil.

Which took forever. What was it about watched pots?

Cora sighed.

Sherry had a small TV in the kitchen for when she cooked. Cora switched it on, caught the end of a reality show where people were trying to lose weight.

"Send 'em over here," Cora muttered.

The eleven o'clock news came on. Becky Baldwin's interview played for the umpteenth time. The Channel Eight news team had no more insight into Mr. Overmeyer's alleged murder than it had when it broke the story that morning. Chief Harper had yet to comment, but Cora could imagine how he felt. It would be a while before Becky Baldwin was back in his good graces.

The water was boiling. Cora dropped in the noodles, got a fork, stirred them around.

Cooking wasn't so hard.

Cora got a dog biscuit, tossed it to Buddy.

The doorbell rang.

Buddy went yapping off in that direction.

Cora frowned.

No one came calling after eleven o'clock. Not in Bakerhaven. It just wasn't done. Who could it be? Harvey Beerbaum? If it was him, his chances of marrying her would have dropped from next to nil to half-past hopeless.

Cora scowled at the door. Apartments in the city had peepholes. In the country, you never knew who was on your front stoop.

She pushed back the blind on the window, peered out.

Standing outside was a man in a stocking cap. That was a bad sign. It wasn't cold enough for a stocking cap.

And Cora didn't know him.

Cora fumbled through her purse, gripped the handle of her pistol. Wondered how she ever got along without a safety chain on the door. She really should install one. Of course, she only ever thought of it in moments she needed it.

Cora opened the door a crack. "Yes?"

"Miss Felton?"

"Yes?"

"I need your help."

"Why?"

"I'm scared."

"How come?"

"Mr. Overmeyer."

"What about him?"

"He was killed."

"How do you know?"

"It was on the news."

"Oh?"

"You gotta help me."

"Why?"

The little man shuffled his feet.

"I'm afraid I'm next."

CHAPTER 12

Cora's visitor sat on the couch. He wore blue jeans, a plaid shirt, a peacoat, and a stocking cap. He was shivering. His eyes were watery, and his nose was running.

"You're cold. You want some tea?"

"No."

"Good. You wouldn't get it. It's late, I'm tired, you got in by saying the magic words. Who are you and what do you want?"

"Stockholm."

"Like the syndrome?"

"Excuse me?"

"Skip it. How do you know Overmeyer?"

"We go way back."

"You don't look old enough."

"He knew my father."

"Where?"

"Is it important?"

"No. I don't feel like cross-examining you. You got a story to tell, tell it."

"Fifty years ago, Overmeyer and my father

were partners."

"In what?"

"An investment."

"What kind of investment?"

"Stock."

"Aha."

"Why do you say that?"

"Nothing. I just have some stocks of my own. I know how volatile the market can be."

"Exactly. Anything you do, you take a chance."

"What happened?"

"It's not like we played the market. We had a little money, we bought some stock, we held on to it."

"What was the stock?"

His eyes flicked. Cora wondered if he was going to lie. Instead, he evaded.

"You know, fifty years ago everybody smoked."

"Tell me about it."

"It looked like everybody always would."

"So?"

"We bought Philip Morris."

"Oh."

"Not a lot. But since then it's split several times."

"So why wasn't Overmeyer rich?"

"He and my father were silent partners.

They didn't hold the stock."

"I don't understand."

"They had the right to the money. It just wasn't in their name."

"What gave them the right?"

"Stock-pooling agreement."

"Do you have it?"

"No."

"Where is it?"

"I don't know."

"Who are the other two partners?"

"That's not important."

"Are they living?"

"That's not important."

"It is to them."

"The stock belongs to them and their descendants. That doesn't matter. The point is, there's four owners. I'm one of them. Overmeyer was another."

"Who's his heir?"

"I have no idea."

"Where's the stock-pooling agreement?"

"Everyone had a copy."

"Where's yours?"

"Mislaid."

"Are you kidding me?"

"When my father died, I could not find it in his papers."

"So you went to Overmeyer."

"No."

"Why not?"

His face showed impatience. "It doesn't matter. You're obsessing about small things. The important thing is if they killed Overmeyer, they could be after me."

"Why are you telling me this?"

"You're smart. You're resourceful. You'll look out for my interests."

"You live in Bakerhaven?"

"Why do you ask?"

"I've never seen you before."

"That's not important."

"It is to me. Where can I reach you?"

"Don't worry. I'll reach you."

Cora put up her hands. "No, no, no. This is utterly wacky. Your father and the dead man were in a partnership with two guys you won't name over a pooling agreement you don't have that leads you to believe whoever killed Overmeyer may be after you?"

He smiled. "Now you've got it."

"So why aren't the other two in danger?"

"I'm sure they are. I just don't care." His nose twitched. "Something burning?"

"Oh, my God! The noodles!"

Cora leapt up, raced into the kitchen.

The water had boiled dry. The noodles were scorching the pan. Wisps of smoke were curling up to the ceiling.

She grabbed the pot, burned her hand, screamed, cursed, dropped the pot. She shut off the fire, snatched up a pot holder, put the pan in the sink, turned on the water. Jumped back from the mushroom cloud of steam that erupted. As it subsided, she shut off the water, assured herself nothing was on fire.

Cora composed herself, went back to her visitor.

He was gone.

CHAPTER 13

Chief Harper looked as if he'd just eaten a bucket of nails instead of one of Mrs. Cushman's blueberry-ginger muffins. "Stock-pooling agreement?"

"Yeah. Can you trace it for me, Chief?"

"Someone named Stockholm bought stock?"

"I admit it's quite a coincidence."

"Yeah. Like Moneymaker winning the poker tournament."

"If the guy's telling the truth, the stock wouldn't be in his name."

"Whose name would it be in?"

"I have no idea."

"That makes it harder to trace."

"Yeah."

"And now I got my own problems. Thanks to Rick Reed and Becky Baldwin, everyone and their brother knows I got a homicide. Even though I haven't officially announced it yet."

"Why don't you?"

"I want to calm down first. So I don't bite somebody's head off. Then you come to me with a stock-pooling story that makes no sense."

"It makes no sense because we don't know the details."

"No," Harper said. "It makes no sense because it doesn't make sense. A ninety-two-year-old man living in squalor and all the time he's got a fortune in stocks squirreled away?"

"Would that be the first rich recluse you ever ran into, Chief?"

"No. But if that's the case, why do you kill him for it? More to the point, why do you kill him for it if you don't get it?"

"We don't *know* no one got it."

"Yes, we do. We know no one *inherited* it. The guy doesn't have a relative within a hundred miles of here. Make that five hundred. The best I can do is a great-nephew from San Antonio who's flying in to settle the estate."

"What estate?"

"Exactly. The guy's got a ramshackle hut on a quarter acre of land. It might be worth twenty or thirty thousand to anyone who wanted to tear down the house and start over. It's hard to imagine this guy from San

86

Antonio doing that. So, unless some other heir pops up, he's likely to turn it over to the local Realtor and go home."

"Twenty or thirty thousand is a nice piece of pocket change."

"Can you see some guy from San Antonio sending his uncle poison candy in the hope of picking it up?"

"Was the poison in candy?"

"I'm not sure what the poison was in."

"From the look on your face, I'd say your coffee. What's the problem, Chief?"

"What's the problem? I've got a motive-less crime with no suspects. Now you bring me some cock-and-bull story about some guy with no name and no address."

"You're the police. I imagine you can get his address."

"Did he come in a car?"

"If I had a license plate number, I'd have given it to you, Chief."

"Did he come in a car?"

"He came right up the walk and knocked on the door."

"Did he come in a car?"

"Damn it, I don't know!" Cora said irritably. "There. You happy? I was cooking when he arrived, I was burning noodles when he left."

"Burning noodles?"

"Don't start with me, Chief. Sherry's gone, I'm on my own. I'm not having an easy time. I'm not used to being on my own."

"You should get married again."

"Is that a proposal? I thought you had a wife and kid."

"What are you going to do when they get home?"

"Eat."

"Are you staying there?"

"No. Sherry can't move in with Aaron's folks. One of us has to go."

"You're moving in with Aaron's folks?"

Cora grimaced. "Go ahead. Make fun. Just because you've got a murder you can't solve."

"You can't either. You didn't even see a car."

"Bite me."

Harper frowned. "If it has to do with stock, what's it got to do with a computer?"

"Maybe it's logged in the computer."

"Hmmm."

"Or the pooling agreement," Cora said. "No one's found his pooling agreement. If it's written up in WordPerfect, you'd just have to print it out. Of course, then it wouldn't be signed." Cora sighed. "Damn. I wish Sherry were here. She knows this stuff.

Like how you scan a document and save it as a TIFF or a JFIF or a JPEG."

"How many shares of stock are we talking about?"

"I don't know."

"What's the company?"

"Philip Morris."

"Oh, my God. Overmeyer's an insider, blowing the whistle on the tobacco companies."

"Right. So they poisoned him with arsenic. They probably put it in his cigarettes. Can you smoke arsenic? I wouldn't think so. Cyanide seems more likely."

"It wasn't cyanide."

"You think I'm serious?"

"I don't know what to think. I'm still upset about Becky Baldwin. Coming in here with a cock-and-bull story."

"Cock-and-bull story?"

"That Dennis is hanging around. I haven't seen him. Have you?"

"You think Becky invented that story to give her an excuse to drop by the police station just on the off chance you had a murder investigation?"

"No. But suppose she knew about it. Suppose she overheard one of Barney Nathan's nurses talking about it over lunch. That's not hard to believe."

"It demonstrates a level of paranoia I wouldn't have expected of you, Chief. Then again, if you really think I hid that gun . . ."

"I didn't say I thought you *hid* the gun. I said I thought you *found* the gun. Before you found it with me."

"That's absurd."

"Why? Because it's the sort of thing you wouldn't do? Actually, it's *exactly* the sort of thing you'd do. You may not have done it in this case. That just means you didn't have the opportunity."

"Am I under arrest?"

"No."

"Good. I didn't think so, but you never know. So, what's with the gun? You traced it yet?"

"Almost."

"What's that mean?"

"We've narrowed it down."

"To what?"

"West Virginia."

"Oh?"

"The serial number matches a shipment of Smith and Wesson revolvers shipped to Rawley's Hardware and Sporting Goods in the summer of 1948."

"Nice work, Chief."

"Thank you. This information might have been more helpful if Rawley's Hardware and Sporting Goods hadn't burned to the ground in 1963."

"After carefully registering every gun sale with the government?"

"Yeah, wouldn't that be nice."

"You mean they didn't?"

"No, they did. The records just don't happen to include Mr. Overmeyer's weapon."

"So it's a dead end?"

"At least a detour. At the moment, we're tracing test bullets fired from Overmeyer's gun against fatal bullets from unsolved homicides."

"How long will that take?"

"You'd have to ask Dan." Harper shook his head. "His last estimate was Christmas."

CHAPTER 14

Becky Baldwin frowned. "What are you talking about?"

"It's not a riddle," Cora told her. "We're just having a conversation. When do you stop looking for something?"

"You mean when do you give up?"

"No, that's not what I mean. Actually, that's one answer. When do you stop looking? When you give up. So what's the other answer?"

"When you find it?" Becky said with ill-suppressed irritation.

"Yes," Cora said. "You stop looking when you find it. That's a real danger in a murder investigation. It's the reason so many innocent people go to jail. The police are looking for a killer, they find him, they stop looking. The fact he isn't the killer doesn't matter. The police have stopped looking."

"That doesn't fit your premise," Becky said.

"What do you mean?"

"You said you stop looking for something when you find it. If the person isn't the killer, then the police haven't found it."

"Exactly," Cora said.

Becky shook her head. "That's semantically incorrect. Somewhat odd, for a woman of your verbal talents."

"Don't be irritating. I'm not playing word games. Just trying to make a point. The police were looking for something. They think they found it, so they stopped looking."

"What are you talking about?"

Cora told Becky about the clues in the crossword puzzle.

Becky frowned. "You were looking for a computer and you found a gun? So you stopped looking?"

"Chief Harper stopped looking."

"Did you point that out to him?"

"I tried. A cursory inspection of the house does not indicate the presence of a computer."

"Does a cursory inspection of the house make the presence of a computer seem likely?"

"Oh."

"Why do you say that?"

"Have you seen Overmeyer's cabin?"

"No. Why?"

"Somehow a computer isn't the first thing that springs to mind."

"What is?"

"A HazMat suit."

"A what?"

"Whatever you call 'em. You know, those bulky space suits when there might be an airborne virus. Like Dustin Hoffman wore in *Outbreak*."

"What?"

"You didn't see it? Probably studying for the bar exam. The point is, I'm going over the place with Chief Harper, we found a gun and stopped looking."

"So?"

"The problem with searching Overmeyer's place is he's only got a quarter of an acre. His neighbors have larger tracts of land, but even so, they're rather close. They'd be apt to see a car parked in a driveway."

"Why are you telling me this?"

"You're a lawyer."

"You want my legal opinion? Butt out."

"I don't want your legal opinion."

"You want me to defend you if you're arrested breaking into the place?"

"Absolutely not."

"I'm glad to hear it. So what do you want

me to do?"

"Help me not get caught."

CHAPTER 15

"I don't like this," Becky said as they drove out of town.

"What's not to like?" Cora told her. "You're just giving me a ride."

"I'm a lawyer. I know the difference between giving someone a ride and being an accessory."

"An accessory to what? I'm just paying a call on my old friend Overmeyer."

"Who happens to be dead."

"He has that character flaw. Aside from that, he's a hell of a guy."

"You'll be careful?"

"Aren't I always?"

"How will I know when to pick you up?"

"You'll hear the police sirens."

"Cora."

"I don't know. I'd call you on my cell phone, if I had one."

"You don't have a cell phone?"

"I don't need one. Except for breaking

96

and entering. Would you advise me to get one just for that?"

Becky tried to give her a withering glance without driving off the road.

"Maybe Overmeyer's phone is still hooked up. I can call you from it."

"Don't you dare! All I need is a record on my cell phone of having gotten a call from a dead man."

"Relax. I don't think Overmeyer even has a phone."

"If he does, promise you won't use it?"

"I might call my bookie. Here, this is it."

Becky drove up the driveway.

Overmeyer's cabin was on a country road where there were houses on only one side of the street. A grove of woods hid the neighbors to the north, but on the property to the south, a two-story Colonial was in plain view.

"So much for sneaking in," Becky said.

"I'm not sneaking in. I'm just not leaving a car parked in front of the cabin to call attention to myself."

"In case the police should drive by."

"Well, it would spoil their day."

"Not to mention mine," Becky said dryly. "When should I pick you up?"

"Uh-oh. Not going to fly."

"What do you mean?"

"Without appearing to stare, look over my shoulder at the neighbor's house. *Without* appearing to stare."

"There's a man on the porch. Looking at us."

"There certainly is. Which changes things. You can't let me out and drive off."

"Should we pretend we just pulled in to turn around?"

"Don't be silly. No one drives all the way up a driveway to turn around."

"I can't help that," Becky said. "It's either that or drop you off."

"No, it isn't."

"What do you mean?"

"Get out of the car."

"Huh?"

"Come on, Nancy Drew. Shut off the engine and get out. I can't sneak in, I've been seen. The only thing to do is walk in like we have every right to be here."

"We have *no* right to be here."

"He doesn't know that. Come on."

Cora got out of the car and walked up to the front door.

Becky sat for a moment in helpless frustration. Then she shut off the engine and joined her.

"Good girl," Cora said. "Wait right here, act bored. Mr. Whoosy-whatsy's still watching us. Don't look at him. I'll let you in."

"Let me in?"

"Unless you want to crawl through the window. You don't want to crawl through the window, do you?"

Cora went around to the back of the house, pushed open the kitchen window she'd managed to unlock when she and Chief Harper were searching the place. With an athletic little hop, quite agile for a woman of more years than she was admitting, Cora squirmed through the window, crawled across the counter, and went to the front door to let in a rather exasperated Becky Baldwin.

"What was that all about?" Becky demanded.

"I had the key to the kitchen door, went around to let you in."

"Really?"

"No, but that's what I hope the neighbor will assume. Provided he didn't see me climbing through the window."

"You broke into the house?"

"Well, how did you think I was going to get in?"

"When I dropped you off in the driveway, I was just an accessory. Now I'm a full-fledged accomplice."

"That's good. It would be a shame to be a

half-fledged accomplice. The girls in maxi-mum security would probably tease you something awful."

"Stop trying to humor me. I'm here, I don't like it, let's get on with it." Becky looked around. "What a dump!"

"Bette Davis. Originally. Quoted by Eliza-beth Taylor in *Who's Afraid of Virginia Woolf? What a dump!*"

"Okay, where did you search?"

"The upstairs closet. That's where we found the gun. In the floorboards under a box of junk."

"How'd you find it?"

"The junk was so worthless there was no reason to keep it except to cover something up."

"Was that your deduction? It certainly *sounds* like you."

"You might pass that on to Chief Harper. He thinks I might have known the gun was there."

"Seriously?"

"I resent it. The idea I might break into a crime scene to look for evidence."

"I can see how that would rankle. Okay, where do we start?"

"Let's start at the bottom and work up. That's the cellar door."

"This place has a cellar?"

"More like a crawl space."

"You didn't search it?"

"The chief did."

"He find anything?"

"An old bicycle." Cora fished a flashlight out of her purse and swung open the door. "After you, my dear."

"Me? You got the flashlight."

"Here."

Becky switched on the flashlight, shone it down the steps. "I don't see why you don't want to — Oh, my God!"

"What is it?"

Becky recoiled, repugnance on her face. "Did the chief tell you what's down here?"

"Rats and spiders."

"That's the polite version. It would appear Mr. Overmeyer's septic system leaks."

"The chief didn't mention that. You see anything down there?"

"You've gotta be kidding."

"No, it's why we came."

"It's why *you* came. I'm the driver."

"Come on, Becky. Hold your nose and take a look."

Becky glared at Cora a moment, then swung the flashlight back down the stairs. "There's a bike."

"I know."

"And mousetraps."

101

"What?"

"There's a row of mousetraps. More like a semicircle."

"Around the bottom of the stair?"

"Sort of. Convex, not concave."

"What are you talking about?"

"I thought you were a linguist. The mouse-traps do not encircle the bottom of the stair, they're like a ball the bottom of the stair is about to kick. Only half, of course."

"Oh, for Christ's sake." Cora took a breath, pushed by Becky to see for herself.

The mousetraps were loosely arranged as Becky had said. All were sprung. None had trapped a mouse.

"I thought he was kidding about the rats," Cora said. She shouldn't have. Her lungs were greeted by a blast of foul air.

She fled the cellar, closed the door. "Okay," she said, brushing spiderwebs from her face. "Let's try the kitchen."

"You think he'd hide something in the kitchen?"

"I have no idea why this bird would do anything."

"And you have no idea why anyone would want to kill him?"

"I wouldn't go that far," Cora said. "I never met the guy, and *I* want to kill him."

"That's not very nice. So he's got busted

plumbing. Aside from that, I'm sure he was a sweet old coot."

"Oh, yeah? Try opening a few of those cabinets."

"Why? Oh, my God!" Becky said, gawking at the moldy, vermin-ridden excuse for food in the cupboard. "Do you suppose he actually ate this stuff?"

"You'd think it would have killed him faster than the arsenic. For the full effect, try the refrigerator."

"I'll forgo the pleasure. I assume you checked the freezer?"

"It doesn't seem to be working. At any rate, there's nothing in it."

Becky surveyed the kitchen cabinets, which stopped about a foot from the ceiling. "Did you look on top of the cabinets?"

"Why, Becky Baldwin, I'm proud of you. Let's have a look."

"I don't suppose there's a stepladder."

"I think we'll have to use a chair." Cora eyed the two at the kitchen table with suspicion. "You'd better do it. I have to get down to fighting weight."

"Fighting weight?"

Cora waggled her hand. "I usually get married about ten pounds less, start eating after the honeymoon."

Becky looked shocked.

"Hey, don't knock it till you've tried it," Cora told her. "When you've had a husband or two, you'll know what I mean."

Becky pulled over a chair, set it in front of the counter next to the refrigerator. She climbed on the seat of the chair, stepped up onto the counter. Peered over the top of the cabinet.

"Anything there?" Cora asked.

"Cobwebs and dust."

"What about the other cabinets?"

Becky looked around the kitchen. "They appear empty, too. There's something on the one over the stove."

"What?"

"Can't tell. It's covered with dust. I have to move the chair."

There was a knock on the front door.

Cora quoted the lyrics from a particularly foul rap song.

"What do we do now?" Becky hissed.

"Get down off that chair, and follow my lead."

Cora opened the front door to reveal the man from the neighbor's porch. He was good-looking, perhaps on the younger side of middle age, brown hair with just a few flecks of gray. Cora couldn't recall seeing him around Bakerhaven, and he was the type of man she'd be apt to remember. She experienced a tingling sensation she hadn't felt for some time.

"Sorry to bother you. I live next door. I don't mean this as rude as it sounds, but, well, what are you doing here?"

Cora positively beamed. "And who could blame you for asking. You must be new in town. I'm Cora Felton. I live here with my niece. Not *here,* I mean in Bakerhaven. And this isn't her. She's on her honeymoon. Not her, my niece. This is Becky Baldwin, attorney-at-law. She's taking an inventory of Mr. Overmeyer's estate prior to probating the will."

He smiled at Becky Baldwin. "You're the executor?"

Cora, not happy to see him smitten with the young attorney, jumped back in. "Of course she is. Unless Overmeyer's great-nephew has some objection to her. Which I can't imagine."

"I can't either. Well, let me know what he intends to do with the property."

"Are you interested in it?" Cora asked.

"Lord, no. But if he's going to put it on the market, I might buy it just to keep some kook from moving in."

"Do you think that's likely?"

"Well, look at the place. Only a kook would live here. So, you're either going to get some wack job who thinks this is the cat's meow, or someone who wants to tear it down and start over. I don't need a construction site next door."

"Of course not," Cora purred.

He cocked his head at Becky Baldwin. "You were on TV."

"Yes."

"Claiming Mr. Overmeyer was murdered."

"It's not me that's making the claim. It's the medical examiner and the police."

"Who would want to kill an old man like that?"

"Did you know him well?" Cora asked.

"Lord, no. I barely knew him. He wasn't the type of guy you'd get to know. I don't mean that as bad as it sounds. But the man didn't want to be neighborly. He just wanted to be left alone."

"Did he have many visitors?"

"I wouldn't know."

"But you can see his house. From your front porch."

"I didn't pay much attention. Frankly, the place is an eyesore. I did my best to pretend it wasn't there." He held out his hand. "I'm George Brooks. I didn't kill him to get his land."

"Give him your card," Cora told Becky.

"Your business card. You got one with you?"

"Of course I do."

"Good, let's have it."

Becky pulled a card out of her wallet, started to hand it over. Cora snatched it. "Pen."

Becky gave her a look, fumbled in her purse. Came out with a ballpoint. Cora snatched that, too, scribbled on the card, handed it over. "There you go. Now you got Becky's office number and my home number. You see anything out of the ordinary, give us a call."

"I certainly will." Brooks nodded, smiled. "Sorry to bother you. Got to get back to my wife."

Cora's face fell a mile.

Chapter 16

"Why did you do that?" Becky hissed.

"Shh," Cora warned. "Wait till he's gone."

"Let's get out of here."

"Why? He already caught us. We might as well stay."

"You had to tell him I'm the attorney for the estate?"

"I had to tell him something. 'We broke in to ransack the place' wasn't going to fly."

"What happens when the relative shows up and doesn't hire me?"

"Who's he gonna hire? You're the only game in town."

"He may have his own lawyer."

"That would be embarrassing."

"Cora."

"You worry too much. You're like Sherry in that respect."

"Like Sherry?"

"Don't get testy. I know she's honeymooning with your guy."

"He's not my guy."

"That sounds like a song title. I think maybe it is."

"Don't think I don't know what you're doing," Becky said.

"What am I doing?"

"You're needling me about my love life so I'll forget about the breaking and entering."

"You have a love life?"

"Look who's talking."

"Touché. I was ready to arm wrestle you for hunky neighbor until he turned out to have a wife. I wonder if he's happily married. Do you handle divorces? Of course you do. You handle everything. Do you think it would be tacky to be the guy's divorce lawyer and make a play for him at the same time?"

"There was something on top of the cabinet," Becky prompted.

"See? I knew you'd prefer breaking and entering."

Becky pulled over a chair, climbed up on the counter, fetched down the object.

It was an empty box.

Cora jerked her thumb. "Let's try upstairs."

The bedroom was just as Cora remembered it, small and filthy.

"What do we do now?" Becky said.

"Ever tossed a bedroom? First we look under the mattress. Then we lift the mattress up and look for slits in the mattress. We look through the dresser, look for things taped to the back or bottoms of drawers. We look under the rug, behind the picture on the wall, which I'm going to hazard a guess is not an original."

The picture of dogs playing poker was not an original. The glass was cracked, and one corner of the frame was sprung. Cora swung it out from the wall.

"Anything behind it?" Becky asked.

"Just a safe."

"You're kidding!"

"Yes, I am." Cora let the picture swing back. "Unless this is a Matisse, it's worthless. Did he do poker-playing dogs?"

"Not that I recall."

Cora hopped off the bed.

There came the sound of tires in the driveway.

"Uh-oh," Cora said.

"Who is it?"

"How the hell should I know?"

"What do we do?"

The bedroom had no windows on the driveway side.

"Come on."

Cora and Becky crept down the stairs. Chief Harper was waiting for them.

CHAPTER 17

Chief Harper was not amused. "All right, what are you doing here?"

Cora smiled. "I was just about to ask you the same thing, Chief. I thought you'd finished with the cabin."

"Yeah, but I've got a right to be here. You two have not."

Cora shook her head. "So Brooks ratted us out? I didn't think he was the type."

"According to him, you're inventorying the estate for Overmeyer's heirs."

"The man is a blabbermouth. That's a shame. He was kind of cute. If married."

Harper steamed through the digression. "Which is somewhat amazing, since Overmeyer's only heir is currently in transit."

"That would make him hard to contact."

"It would if it weren't for cell phones. I reached him in Chicago. He denies hiring *anyone* to conserve his estate."

"Oh."

"How about it, Becky? Did this guy hire you?"

"You can't expect her to have that information at her fingertips," Cora said. "She'll have to check her client list and get back to you."

"Since her number of clients usually ranges from one to zero, that shouldn't be too hard."

"Hey, I resent that," Becky said.

"Resent all you like. Do you happen to recall the client? The one you're conducting the inventory for?"

"You shouldn't end a sentence with a preposition, Chief," Cora said. "It's something you should be careful of."

"You mind telling me what you're doing here?"

"In the house of a man we just found out was poisoned?" Cora shrugged. "Can't think of a thing."

"George Brooks is new in town, and clearly not used to your casual approach to the law."

"Oh, yeah? Well, he's awfully eager to buy the dead man's estate. Did he happen to mention that?"

"You're claiming that's a motive for murder?"

"It's better than any you've got."

Harper controlled himself with an effort. He took a breath. "So, did you find anything?"

"Mousetraps," Cora said.

"Huh?"

"In the cellar. There's mousetraps."

"Yes, I was down there."

"You didn't mention mousetraps."

"I said rats and spiders."

"I thought you were trying to scare me."

"I was."

"I mean I thought you were making it up."

"You find anything else?"

"The sewer pipe's broken."

"Relating to the crime."

"How do you know someone didn't kill him for having a broken sewer pipe?"

"Okay. Enough shenanigans. I got a murder to solve. And I can't solve it if I've got to spend all my time chasing you around. In case I wasn't clear before, let me be explicit. This cabin is off-limits. Don't go in, don't drive by it, don't look in the window, don't inventory anything that might happen to be there. And for God's sake, don't remove anything from the property under penalty of death. You haven't removed anything from the property, have you?"

"Absolutely not," Cora said.

"Or do you have anything on your person right now that you intend to take from the property?"

"Gosh, you have a suspicious mind, Chief."

"You agreed just a little too readily."

"There's no pleasing you, Chief. I agree with you, you're unhappy. I don't agree with you, you're unhappy. What do you want us to do?"

"What do I want you to do?" Chief Harper cocked his head. "I want you to avoid any TV interviews in which you give out information not already released by the police."

"Becky must have misunderstood you, Chief. I don't know how that happened."

"Yeah. Well, this time let there be no mistake. I want you to get in your car, drive off, and don't come back here for any reason whatsoever. Is that clear?"

Cora patted him on the cheek. "Crystal."

CHAPTER 18

As soon as Becky dropped her off, Cora hopped in her car and sped back to the cabin. The front door was locked, but the kitchen window was still open. Shimmying through was a pain. It also upped the chance Brooks would call the cops, but that couldn't be helped.

Cora went straight to the bedroom, stood up on the bed, lifted down the picture frame. Recalling lines from the Dylan song about looking like Robert Ford but feeling like Jesse James did not cheer her. She glanced over her shoulder for potential assassins. Finding none, she flopped the picture down on the bed, pulled off the folded piece of paper taped to the back of the dog art. She rehung the picture, pelted down the stairs, and was out of there faster than you could say elderly housebreaker.

Cora felt bad about holding out on Becky. She wouldn't have held out on Sherry, if her niece had been the one helping her search the cabin. To a certain extent, Cora realized that was why she'd done it. She felt guilty about using Becky in Sherry's absence. It was as if Sherry had gotten married so Cora had gotten a surrogate niece. Not exactly, the pilfered paper said. Withholding the evidence kept Becky outside the pale.

Cora raced into the house, locked the front door behind her, as if that would keep Chief Harper out. It kept Buddy in, and he wasn't happy about it, yipping his displeasure until Cora threw him a dog biscuit to shut him up.

Cora flopped her purse on the kitchen table, yanked out her precious find. It was a single sheet of paper folded into eighths. The Scotch Tape was still on. Four strips diagonally across the corners. Cora pulled them off with a reasonable amount of care for her level of excitement.

She unfolded the paper.

There was writing on it, which became evident only when it started to unfold. That was good because any writing on the outside would have been ripped off by the tape. But the writing was on an interior fold. It couldn't be seen when the paper was folded in eighths or quarters, only when it was unfolded into halves.

Cora spun the paper around.

```
. 9 .    . . .    . . .
5 . .    . . .    . 4 .
. 7 8    . . .    . . 6

. . .    . . .    . 5 .
. 3 .    . . 6    1 . .
. 1 .    . . 7    9 . 8

. 8 .    . 4 .    . . 7
. . 1    6 3 .    . . 5
. . 6    1 . .    2 . .
```

It wasn't a message. It was merely numbers. Numbers and dots scrawled on the page in a haphazard fashion. To a woman whose husband had played the ponies — for the life of her, Cora couldn't remember which husband — it looked like some bookie's scratch sheet, a secret record of bets and races the cops could never figure out that made sense only to him.

Or made no sense at all.

Cora sighed.

Was this what she'd risked Chief Harper's wrath for?

Of course not. The numbers weren't the message. Overmeyer had scrawled his message on the *back* of an old piece of paper because he didn't have a *clean* piece of paper. Probably hadn't in years. The message was on the other side.

Cora turned over the paper.

Groaned.

It was a crossword puzzle.

Across

1 Pre-op wash
5 "Zorba the Greek" setting
10 Indian king
14 Juno, to the Greeks
15 Crude carrier
16 Four Corners state
17 Start of a message

19 Old TV clown
20 Kind of point
21 Nervously excited
23 Reactionaries of 1917
26 Beach color
27 Wheel rotator
28 Large cask
29 Is down with
32 Hum or seethe
35 Part 2 of message
38 Blow one's mind
40 Big gobbler
41 Impressive spread
42 Part 3 of message
45 Vegas calculation
46 E. Lansing school
47 Mensa high marks
48 Sukiyaki ingredient
50 Good name for a cook?
51 "The Hustler" locale
55 Executed First World War spy
59 Pushover school course
60 Snobbish attitude
61 Part 4 of message
64 Holiday season, for short
65 Davy Jones's locker
66 Downwind, nautically
67 Early Cosby series
68 Wipe again
69 Cassandra, for example

Down

1 Comic interjection
2 Moves, in realtor lingo
3 "Fear of Flying" author Jong
4 Britney Spears photographers
5 Miler Sebastian
6 Ipanema's city
7 Graceland's former resident
8 Adolescent
9 Galley goof
10 Apply, as cream
11 All-inclusive
12 Charlie Parker's music
13 "Hi, sailor!"
18 1,059 another way
22 Tucker who sang "Strong Enough to Bend"
24 School-zone sign
25 Tithe amounts
28 Ketchup ingredient
29 Like some candy
30 Part of U.S.N.A.
31 "The _____ the limit!"
32 Toto's creator
33 "Ball!" callers
34 Early film actress Pitts
36 Sock part
37 Loud hubbubs
39 Archie Bunker's wife

43 0 degrees latitude
44 "Cock-a-doodle-_____"
49 Went by plane
50 In-your-face style
51 Pierced
52 "Oh, look _____" (shopper's remark)
53 Paris school
54 West Coast NBA hoopster
55 60's–70's dress
56 Intentions
57 Bend in a sink's pipe
58 Marathon, for one
62 Hearing aid
63 Whatever amount

CHAPTER 19

On her way to the police station, Cora bumped into Harvey Beerbaum.

"Well, what do we do now?" he said.

"What do you mean?"

"I solved the puzzle and a man is dead."

"I don't think it's cause and effect."

"Don't be silly. Mr. Overmeyer was murdered. The puzzle is a valuable clue."

"You solved it."

"Yes, but I don't know what it means."

"Join the club."

"How can you be so calm about this? We're involved in a murder."

"Maybe you are, Harvey. I have an alibi."

He looked shocked. "You're joking. Please tell me you're joking."

"I'm joking."

"How can you joke about a thing like that?"

"Make up your mind, Harvey. You just told me to say I was joking."

"Have you talked to Chief Harper?"

"Yes, have you?"

"What does he think?"

"That's what I want to know."

"I asked you first."

"He thinks it has something to do with the puzzle."

"You're kidding!"

"Okay, he *doesn't* think it has something to do with the puzzle."

"Cora."

"I don't know what you want me to say, Harvey. But you solved the puzzle. Surely you noticed all the references to computers in it."

"What?"

"You didn't notice? Well, take another look. I have no idea what it means, but if you think of anything, let me know."

"There was nothing in the puzzle."

"That's what I would have said, too. But the man is dead."

"My goodness."

Harvey hurried off, no doubt to look at the puzzle.

Cora felt bad for deceiving him. And for not trusting him. It was one thing to let him solve a puzzle when it didn't mean anything. And before she knew it was a murder. It was something else to let him solve a puzzle she'd pilfered from a crime scene under the eyes of the cops. It simply wouldn't do. He would have too many scruples. He would have a nervous breakdown. He would want to go to the police.

He would make her life a living hell.

No, there was no way Harvey was getting a look at the puzzle.

Of course, she couldn't show it to Chief Harper, either. She couldn't admit she had it. And he'd just want her to solve it. Assuming he didn't throw her in jail.

Cora hurried down to the police station just in time to meet Overmeyer's heir.

CHAPTER 20

Harmon Overmeyer was a sniveling little man with a nasal voice, a receding chin, a protruding stomach, and a habit of popping his knuckles that set Cora's teeth on edge. He was, in fact, so unattractive a specimen of manhood that Cora had not the least inclination to marry him.

"I came as soon as I could," Harmon declared somewhat defensively. No one had asked him why he hadn't come earlier. "My flight was canceled. Out of San Antonio. They couldn't get me to Washington on time to make the connection. Even rerouting me through Chicago."

"You couldn't get a direct flight?" Cora asked.

Harmon, who had addressed his remark to Chief Harper, looked at her in annoyance. So did Chief Harper.

"Horrible delays all over. It's the terrorists, you know."

Cora didn't really agree. In her opinion, terrorists were too easy a catchall excuse for everything.

"Anyway, we're glad you're here," Harper said. "You'll want to take charge of the estate and arrange for the burial."

"When you spoke to me on the phone, you had not yet found the will."

"We still haven't."

"Have you checked with the town attorney?"

"Ms. Baldwin is the town attorney. Your uncle never consulted her."

"Would that be the young lady I supposedly hired to conserve my estate?"

"Which young lady did you hire?" Cora asked.

"I didn't hire a young lady."

"You hired a man?"

"I didn't hire anyone. I didn't know there was an estate until I got a phone call."

"That was from me," Chief Harper said.

"Yes. Telling me my great-uncle had been murdered. Which was a bit of a shock. I didn't know I *had* a great-uncle. I didn't know he was alive. I didn't know he was dead. I certainly didn't know he'd been murdered. And I don't see why he's *my* responsibility."

"You're his closest living relative."

"Surely he had a closer living relative."

"Do *you* have any living relatives?"

"Not anymore."

Harper frowned.

"Then I'm summoned here to take charge of the estate. Before I even arrive, you call me again to tell me someone has *taken* charge of the estate. In my behalf."

Cora Felton bit the bullet, smiled, batted her eyes. "That was a misunderstanding."

Harmon was having none of it. "Just *how* could that be a misunderstanding?"

"Ms. Baldwin is the only lawyer in town. When anyone dies, she's the conservator of their estate, unless they've made other arrangements. Since Overmeyer had no living relatives —"

"I'm his relative."

"Yes," Cora conceded. "But you didn't even know it. If the chief hadn't dug you up through some good old-fashioned detective work, your great-uncle's property would have wound up being sold at public auction. After being inventoried by the conservator. Who would be Ms. Baldwin."

"Oh, really? If everything was so aboveboard, why did the chief here call me to see if I had actually hired the attorney in question?"

"I can't speak for the chief," Cora said,

speaking for him, "but I would assume that was to ask if you wanted anything out of the ordinary done in light of the fact that your relative appeared to have been murdered."

Harmon turned on the chief. "Would that be the reason?"

Cora put up her hands. "I think we are losing sight of the fact that we have a murder investigation. The point is not who authorized what. The point is who killed your great-uncle."

Harmon favored Cora with a superior smirk. "And just who are you?"

"I'm sorry. This is Cora Felton," Chief Harper said. "You might know her as the Puzzle Lady. She's an amateur detective who's often been invaluable in my investigations."

"Puzzle? What do you mean, puzzle?"

"She has a crossword puzzle column."

"Oh, for goodness' sakes! I thought you were a police matron, someone who searched female prisoners. I thought that was the rather tenuous excuse for your presence. Are you telling me you have none?"

"Watch it, buster. Just because you're rude doesn't mean you're not guilty."

"I beg your pardon?"

"Someone sent your great-uncle poison

chocolates. It might have been you."

"The poison was in chocolates?"

Harper put up his hand. "We're not giving out any information."

"She just did. What's this about chocolates?"

"There's nothing about chocolates," Chief Harper said irritably. "Miss Felton was using that as an example. As a figure of speech. No one is saying the poison was administered in chocolates, and we would thank you not to venture such a theory."

"Now you're trying to gag me?"

"It's a temptation," Cora muttered.

"What was that?"

"Of course I'm not trying to gag you," Chief Harper said. "You can tell the press anything you please. I'm just suggesting for your own good you might want to steer clear of irresponsible statements people might tend to pounce on, give you grief for. Just a friendly hint."

"I'm glad to see you're friendly. I think I can take care of myself. Are you telling me you have no information on the crime?"

"Not at the present, no."

"What about the assessment of the estate?"

"I made no such assessment."

"You allowed a lawyer to."

Chief Harper was keeping his temper with difficulty. "I was not aware of an inventory being made. When it was brought to my attention, I immediately asked if you had authorized it."

"And put a stop to it?"

"Yes."

"You stopped the lawyer in mid-inventory?"

Chief Harper hesitated.

"You *didn't* stop her in mid-inventory?"

"She had already stopped."

"Had she completed her inventory?"

"You'd have to ask her."

"You didn't ask her if she'd completed her inventory?"

"It wasn't high on my list of questions."

"You sound facetious, Officer. Are you being facetious?"

"It's entirely possible. I'm just sitting here having stuff dumped in my lap from all directions. You come here from San Antonio to bawl me out for not keeping a closer eye on the effects of a distant dead relative you didn't even know you had, I am not going to take that kindly. I hope you see my position."

"I hope you see mine. If I'm the principal heir, no matter how remote the relationship, I want what's coming to me."

"Oh, you'll get what's coming to you all right," Cora muttered.

"What was that?"

Harper stepped between them. "If you want your inheritance, then you'll do everything you possibly can to help me clean up this unfortunate situation."

"That's how you see it? As an unfortunate situation?"

"Well, it's hardly a fortunate one," Cora said. "Now, unless you'd like to confess to this crime, why don't you get the hell out of here so Chief Harper and I can solve it."

CHAPTER 21

"Well, would you believe that," Cora said when she'd finally succeeded in throwing Overmeyer's heir out of the office.

Chief Harper looked a little dazed. "Huh?"

"The nerve of that man. I'm surprised you didn't pin his ears back."

"That might have been easier to do if he weren't right. Why were you and Becky Baldwin snooping around the cabin?"

"*Snooping* is such an unpleasant word, Chief. Almost sexist, don't you think?"

"How is that sexist?"

"It implies women."

"Women snoop?"

"That's what it implies."

"If it *implies* it because they *do* it, what's wrong with that?"

"Just because something's true doesn't mean it's not sexist."

Chief Harper put up his hands. "Stop it. We're not having this conversation. You're not getting out of this so easily. What were you and Becky Baldwin doing in the cabin?"

"Looking for evidence you missed."

"I *knew* you were going to say that."

"Then you're not disappointed."

"Did you find it?"

"Of course not."

"Why not?"

"Because you're a thorough investigator, and you didn't miss anything."

"Why do I find that answer so exasperating?"

Cora tactfully changed the subject. "I notice you didn't mention any guns you might be tracing."

"No one asked me about any guns."

"It would seem to come under the heading of Mr. Overmeyer's possessions."

"It would also come under the heading of evidence in a murder investigation. As such, I would prefer not to have it bandied about."

"Did you notice how I carefully didn't bring it up?"

"If you had, I'd have arrested you on the spot."

"I had a feeling," Cora said.

"We have a dead man. We have no apparent motive for his death. Unless some partner in crime wanted to shut him up for some past transgression."

"Or the offspring of such accomplice. You're not about to give Harmon a free ride, are you, Chief?"

"Just between you and me, I'd love to pin it on him."

"Too bad he was in Texas at the time."

"Candy could be sent in the mail."

"Not without wrapping. Big problem there, Chief. You send the guy a box of candy with a note that says, 'Burn the wrapping paper before you eat this,' he's gonna get suspicious."

"True, but if no one suspects he's being poisoned . . ."

"The evidence get cleaned up before you got to it?"

"I didn't say that."

"You didn't have to. This is a mess."

"You're telling me? I got absolutely nothing to go on. I got this bozo running around making trouble. I got Rick Reed asking stupid questions that make *me* look stupid because I got no answer. Yes, I didn't treat Overmeyer's cabin as a crime scene. Because it wasn't a crime scene until two days after he died. If I treated every death as a potential homicide, it would be cruel and heartless. Can you imagine me striding into some new widow's home: 'Hello, ma'am, sorry your husband just kicked the bucket, but it's my job to make sure you didn't hurry him along. You wanna give me your fingerprints and stay out of the bedroom while my boys give it the once-over.' "

"I see your point."

"I'm in a pickle. Unless Dan comes through with the gun, I got nothing."

"Yeah."

"So if you can come up with anything, anything at all, it would be a lifesaver."

"I'll see what I can do," Cora said.

The crossword puzzle was burning a hole in her purse.

CHAPTER 22

Sherry Carter stood on the seat and stuck her head out of the open top as the Land Rover bumped its way across the plains of the Masai Mara. The elephants off to the right, so exciting the first day of the safari, were no big deal. Not since they'd had a herd surround their Jeep. One had even charged before Jonathan, their guide and driver, started the engine and scared him away.

Giraffes were grazing right by the road. Jonathan barely slowed down. Sherry and Aaron had seen enough giraffes to last a lifetime. Today they were after wildebeests.

The migration this year had been late. There'd been ample rainfall in the Serengeti, grazing had been good, and the wildebeests had been slow to move. A two-week delay would be enough for Aaron and Sherry to miss them. They couldn't have that. If the wildebeests wouldn't come to them, they'd go to the wildebeests. Even if they had to drive all the way to Tanzania.

Aaron put his arm around Sherry's shoulders. "Do you know why the wildebeests aren't in Kenya yet?"

She frowned. "Why?"

Aaron's eyes twinkled. "Because the rain in the plain stays mainly in Tanzania."

Sherry batted at him playfully with her binoculars, and they wrestled around in the back of the Land Rover.

"Easy, tiger lady," Aaron said, laughing and pinning her hands. "You know, we don't have to do this."

Sherry grinned. "I promised you a wildebeest, I'm going to give you a wildebeest."

"I can live without a wildebeest."

"You say that now. But when we get home . . ."

"I'd settle for a reticulated giraffe."

"Who wouldn't? But we've seen enough giraffes."

"You can never see enough giraffes."

"Well, we're not going to turn back now. It's wildebeests or bust."

"Speaking of bust . . ."

"Why, Aaron Grant. Was that a racy Cora remark?"

"That wasn't the way I saw it."

"Well, you watch your mouth. I'm a married lady."

"So I recall."

"Look!" cried Jonathan. "Wildebeest!"

The Land Rover bumped over a small rise, and there they were. Thousands of wildebeests, as far as the eye could see.

"Wow," Aaron murmured.

"Worth it?"

"I'll say."

Jonathan assured them this was nothing. In the height of the migration, the plain would be solid wildebeests. Millions of them.

Sherry and Aaron were happy to settle for tens of thousands. After all, they were on their honeymoon.

They got back to camp just before dinner.

The tents they lived in were large, had electricity and running water. Not that you could drink it, but you could take a heated shower. The tent flaps had to be knotted shut securely so the monkeys didn't get in.

The bar and dining room, with thatched roof and open air, and warthogs trotting freely in the yard, still featured a battery-charging station and Internet access port.

Sherry took her iTouch out of her pocket, logged on.

"I thought you weren't going to do that," Aaron said.

"I'm just picking up my e-mail."

"I thought that's what you weren't going to do."

"I'm not going to *answer* my e-mail. That doesn't mean I can't pick it up."

"What's the use of picking it up if you aren't going to answer it?"

"Just to make sure nothing's wrong."

"Nothing's wrong. Cora has your international cell phone number. In an emergency, she'd call."

"She might forget how."

"You wrote it down for her."

"Sweetheart. It's Cora. You know what convoluted logic might make her decide not to call."

"I know what convoluted logic might make you decide to check your e-mail."

"I'm not going to check it every day. Just every half a million wildebeests."

"Wasn't that something?"

"I'll say. . . . Ah. I picked up a signal. And look. Four new messages."

"Only four?"

"I have a good spam filter."

"Even so. When was the last time you checked your e-mail?"

"What's the big deal?"

"Sherry."

"So, I checked it last night. We didn't have

anything. Just junk. And today we got —
Uh-oh!"

"What?"

"Cora."

"What does she want?"

"I don't know, but she sent an attachment."

"Cora sent an attachment?"

"I left instructions."

"What does she say?"

Sherry read, " 'Didn't want to bother you, but I got this puzzle. I gave the first one to Harvey, which was okay because it didn't mean anything, and he solved it for Chief Harper. Now I got another one, and I can't give it to Harvey because Chief Harper doesn't know about it because I found it at a crime scene where I wasn't supposed to be. I'm hoping it means nothing and I can throw it in the trash. But old man Overmeyer, the geezer with the cabin, got himself poisoned, and I could use a little help. If you can solve this puzzle and send it back, I'd be grateful, and if you happen to notice any way it might relate to a thirty-two-caliber Smith and Wesson revolver, that would be even better. Have a happy honeymoon. Don't let the monkeys steal your undies. Cora.' "

"The monkeys steal your undies?"

"An old South African toast." Sherry smiled. "I'm surprised you haven't heard it."

CHAPTER 23

Cora glowered at the puzzle and considered Overmeyer the most annoying, stupid, idiotic, exasperating man she'd ever met. And she'd never met him. But he ranked right up there with some of the ones she'd married. The man deserved to die a thousand painful, gruesome deaths. Arsenic was too good for him. Surely something more diabolical could have been planned for the dead man from hell.

Cora gnashed her teeth and looked at the dead man's puzzle.

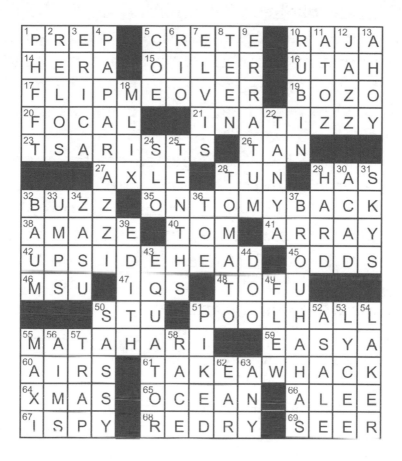

The theme entry read: "Flip me over onto my back. Upside head take a whack."

Boy, if the son of a bitch were only here, Cora would take such a whack. The two poems had to be the worst meaningless drivel she'd ever encountered. "At noon I can not be done. So I should try to at one." And "Flip me over onto my back. Upside head take a whack." It should at least be

"Upside *my* head." Probably didn't fit. Or maybe he was afraid she'd do it and wanted to maintain deniability. "No, not *my* head. Did I say *my* head? I didn't say *my* head. How about *his* head? Take a whack at *his* head, if you want."

Cora had been so eager to get the puzzle back from Sherry. At the same time, she had been conflicted about the possible result. If it meant anything, she'd have to take it to Chief Harper. Which she could get away with if it was important enough. If it was dropping a significant clue in his lap. The theft of the puzzle would be forgiven in exchange for unveiling the culprit.

On the other hand, if the puzzle was meaningless, she didn't have to show it to Chief Harper. In fact, she *couldn't* show it to Chief Harper. It would be suicide to show it to Chief Harper. If the poem was meaningless, she would keep quiet and pretend it never happened.

Well, there it was, and if there was a meaning hidden within it, Cora wouldn't know it. Nor would any other sane, rational person on the face of the earth. Which wasn't fair. If the guy was going to hide the damn thing behind his poker-playing-dogs picture, it ought to mean something.

Only it didn't.
It really wasn't fair.

CHAPTER 24

Cora Felton saw him as she came out of Cushman's Bake Shop. He ducked back into the shadows, but that was what gave him away. Cora was always on the alert for elusive surveillance tactics. Not that she was often followed, but when she was, she knew it.

In this case, she knew the shadow. Becky Baldwin was right. The man snooping around was none other than Sherry Carter's worthless ex-husband.

So. Dennis Pride was watching her. Had he followed her to the bake shop? Or just spotted her going in and waited for her to come out?

Cora was tempted to grab him by the scruff of the neck and demand to know what he was doing. But he'd probably lie. And then she'd waste her time figuring out what he was doing, why he was lying, and the whole nine yards. It was easier just to see for herself.

She hopped into her red Toyota, backed out of her parking spot, and drove slowly out of town. In the rearview mirror, she could see a black sedan pull away from the curb and follow. Cora went by the gas station, took a left on Holcomb Road. The sedan put on its blinker. Cora grinned in satisfaction, stepped on the gas, hurtled down the road. After a few seconds, she took her foot off the accelerator, let the engine slow the car. The Toyota had gone from twenty to eighty to thirty in the wink of an eye, and when the black sedan came into view, Cora was driving safely within the speed limit, though way down the road. It occurred to her that it would be really neat if Dennis had been smoking dope. After all, the guy was in a rock band, and if he was really stoned, her car seeming to teleport ahead would be a weird trip.

Cora was coming up on Overmeyer's cabin. To her right was George Brooks's house, a mansion by comparison. She could barely see it from the road. The driveway disappeared amid oak and maple trees. It was only from the cabin one had a direct view. Cora figured Brooks would plant bushes or hedges as soon as he got around to it. Assuming he couldn't buy the land.

Cora slowed as she reached the cabin but didn't turn in the drive. She went on by, pulled up at the side of the road, parked by the grove of trees. She slid across the front seat, slipped out the passenger door, dropped to the ground, and began crawling through the underbrush back toward the cabin. It was rough going. Her drawstring purse kept snagging on bushes and branches. But she wasn't about to leave it in the car. It had her smokes and her gun. She wasn't sure which she needed more.

The black sedan had pulled over just past the driveway to the cabin. Cora approached from the passenger side, yanked open the door, slid into the front seat. "Hello, Dennis."

Cora had wanted to blow his mind, and she wasn't disappointed. Dennis could not have looked more surprised if his guitar had vanished in midset. He gawked at Cora, his mouth open. He wore a suit and tie, and his long hair was slicked back. It was his salesman's costume, his guise as the hardworking son-in-law of Norman Wallenstein, president and CEO of Wallenstein Textiles.

"Not much to say, huh? Strong, silent type. I usually like that in a man. In your case, I'll make an exception."

"What are you doing here?"

Cora frowned, shook her head. "Oh. Bad question. Just the worst. I *live* here. I have a *right* to be here. Unlike some people."

"I have a right to be here."

"You mean because Sherry's gone? On her honeymoon?"

Dennis winced, scowled.

"You may have a *right* to be here. You don't have a *reason*. And I think Brenda Wallenstein Pride, your current wife, the one who *hasn't* divorced you yet, would bear me out on that. So if you haven't any reason to be here, what the hell are you doing following me around?"

"I wasn't following you around."

"Well, you were doing a pretty good impression of it. Going where I go. Stopping where I stop. Waiting to see what I do."

"Maybe I just wanted to see the cabin."

"Huh?"

"There was a murder here. Or hadn't you heard?"

"Yes. There was a murder at the cabin. That's back there, Dennis. You drove right by it."

"So did you."

"I thought you weren't following me."

"That doesn't mean I don't know your car."

"Give it up, Dennis. Sherry's married."

"So am I."

"Yes, you are. Now, that may not mean anything to you, but it does to her. You're out of her life. You've got no business here."

"I'd like to solve the crime."

That caught Cora up short. "I beg your pardon?"

"You got no idea who killed him, do you? No one does. No more than I do. It's up for grabs. Figuring it out. It's important. It's what a responsible person would do."

"Too bad you don't fall into that category."

Dennis smiled. "I understand your attitude. This is your territory, you don't want anyone treading on your space. But we're after the same thing. We both want this killer caught. What do you say we pool our information."

Cora stared at him. There was a glint in his eye that never came from liquor or cocaine. She knew it well. The sign of obsession so great that logic and reason would not prevail. The man could only be dealt with like an obstinate three-year-old determined to have his own way.

Instead of laughing in his face, Cora said, "What information do you wanna pool?"

"You first."

She took a breath. "Overmeyer was most

likely poisoned."

"That's not news."

"It isn't official."

"It may be unofficial, but everyone knows."

"Well, now it's confirmed. Your turn."

Dennis shook his head. "Huh-uh. You tell me something no one knows, I'll tell you what I know. Otherwise, forget it."

Cora glared at him in contempt.

"Consider it forgotten," she said, and climbed out of the car.

CHAPTER 25

"Your client's insane."

Becky Baldwin raised her eyebrows. "What else is new?"

"I'm not kidding. He's certifiable. It's a real problem."

"Tell me something I don't know."

Cora snorted in exasperation. Becky Baldwin's law office was over the pizza parlor, and aromas had a tendency to seep up. Today's special was the supreme combo — chicken, sausage, and pepperoni. Cora would rather have been eating it than discussing Dennis Pride.

"It's worse than usual. He's snapped. He thinks he's an amateur detective, trying to solve the crime before the cops."

Becky smiled. "A sure sign of dementia."

Cora suggested uses for Becky's law books unlikely to have helped her pass the bar.

"What are you getting so pissed about? He's my client."

"Exactly, and you can't control him. He's on probation, and here he is running around making trouble."

"Unfortunately, he's within his rights."

"He may be within his rights, but he's out of his mind. I mean more than usual. I don't know how to get through to you if you're not going to take this seriously."

"I'm taking it seriously. What do you want me to do?"

"Bring him in. Give him a talking-to."

"I do that every week."

"This time make an impression."

"How?"

"I don't know. Wear your black leather dominatrix outfit. Just make him listen."

"How do you know about my dominatrix outfit?"

"Are you kidding?"

"Yeah."

"Damn. All right, listen. Dennis claims he knows something."

"You think he does?"

"I have no idea. But he won't tell me unless I tell him something first."

"Which you won't do?"

"I'd rather be staked naked to an anthill."

"Yeah, but you do that every week."

"My, you've gotten feisty since your boyfriend got married."

"Thank you."

"So how about it? Think you can work your wiles on Dennis?"

"I'd rather be staked naked to an anthill."

"Good point."

"Well, speaking entirely as a lawyer, it occurs to me if Dennis doesn't want to tell us what he knows, there's not much we can do about it."

"Right."

"On the other hand, if he doesn't tell Chief Harper, he'd be guilty of withholding evidence, compounding a felony, and conspiring to conceal a crime."

Cora smiled.

"For a Barbie doll, you have a keen legal mind."

CHAPTER 26

Chief Harper's office was filled with Over-meyer heirs. It was a veritable bonanza. The day before, he'd had only one. Today, there were no fewer than five clamoring for attention.

Cora stuck her head in the door. "Am I interrupting?"

Chief Harper looked as though he'd just been thrown a lifeline. "Not at all. Come right in. These people were just leaving."

A truculent gentleman in a three-piece suit took exception to the statement. "Leaving? I just got here. I have no intention of leaving until I find out what happened to my cousin."

"*Second* cousin," a middle-aged man corrected. His plaid jacket and red toupee clashed to the point of causing headaches, if not seizures.

The woman with him might have been drawn by Charles Addams. "Twice removed," she sneered.

Since no introductions were forthcoming, Cora dubbed them Bozo and Cruella.

A blond woman in fishnet stockings and more makeup than the average chorus line batted her eyes at no one in particular. "It's just so very sad." Who she was and why it was sad for her were not readily apparent; still, if the woman wanted to think so, Cora couldn't blame her for it. She *could* blame her for the makeup, which was simply god-awful. She looked like a hooker. Not necessarily female.

"Harumph," said an elderly gentleman in the pack. At least that's what Cora assumed he was saying. The actual noise might have been produced by yodeling with a collapsed lung. The man wore a white shirt buttoned to the neck and tan slacks belted to the armpits. He was shorter than Cora, which made him about four-fifths pants.

The Geezer, as Cora dubbed him, had captured her attention with his "harumph." She waited for more. None was forthcoming. Apparently, he figured harumph covered the situation.

"Just a darn minute," Bozo said. "I feel we've been gotten here under false pretenses. We show up for the reading of the will. No one said anything about a murder."

"And there's no damn will," the pinstripe-suited man whined. Cora dubbed him Cranky Banker. "How do you like them apples? It's up to us to sort the whole thing out."

"Oh, yeah?" Cruella said. "As if that'll happen now. It's a murder. What do you think happens in those cases? They cut up the estate while they're looking for the killer? I don't think so. Isn't that right, Officer?"

"It's not my place to discuss the disposition of the estate."

"Well, whose place is it? That's what I want to know. Who's the gentleman's attorney?"

"By 'the gentleman,' you mean your dear departed uncle Overmeyer?" Cora put in.

"Who the hell are you?" Cruella demanded. "You better not be his sister. I know for a fact he had no sisters."

There were many ways to Cora's heart, but suggesting she might be the sister of an nonagenarian was not one of them. She cocked her head at Chief Harper. "Have you checked their alibis?"

That triggered an outburst of sputtered protests.

"Alibis?" Harper said.

"These people seem far too interested in

the estate. One wonders if there might be something worth inheriting."

"There's no reason we should have to supply alibis," Cruella said indignantly. "We were in Green Bay yesterday."

"Look at that," Cranky Banker said. "She says there's no reason to supply alibis and immediately supplies one. I would look at her very closely if I were you."

"Thanks for the advice," Chief Harper said dryly. "Now, if you'd all just run along. Leave your names, addresses, and local contact numbers with the young officer at the desk."

Chief Harper had barely got the gaggle of heirs out of the office before Dan Finley burst in to say he'd traced the bullet.

CHAPTER 27

Chief Harper squinted at the jumble of indecipherable chicken scratches on Dan Finley's notepad. "I can't read this. Where's the paperwork?"

"It's coming. They have to dig it up and copy it."

"Can you read this?"

"Of course." Dan picked up the pad. "Nineteen fifty-four. Convenience store robbery in Mobile, Alabama. Though they probably didn't call them convenience stores back then. Just a roadside gas station that sold beer and soda. Probably a few groceries. Potato chips and the like."

"Dan," Chief Harper prompted.

"Two guys robbed the place and shot the owner dead. Guy went for his gun. Bad move. Probably didn't have more than a hundred bucks in the till. Of course, it was worth more back then —"

"Dan."

"Sorry. Just want you to get the picture. The robbers came out of the store as two innocent bystanders were going in." Dan turned the notepad sideways, ran his finger over some pencil marks that appeared Japanese. "Claude Barnes and Mickey Dare. Just happened to be in the wrong place at the wrong time. They stopped for gas, heard the shots, saw two men come running out. One of the men opened fire, shot 'em both. Hopped in the car and escaped. They were never found. Though one of the witnesses survived and when he recovered, he gave a pretty good description of the men in that car."

"He didn't get the license plate number?" Harper asked.

"According to the cops, it's a miracle he got anything at all. Shot in the chest. Lucky to be alive. He managed to crawl over, try to help his buddy before he passed out. No use. Stone dead, shot in the heart. Cops found the two of them lying together next to a storm drain. Blood was actually running down the drain. How do you like that? Crime's over fifty years old, but some details they still remember. The blood running down the drain."

"I get the symbolism," Chief Harper said dryly. "I wasn't planning on writing a book.

Where does the gun come in?"

"Ah," Finley said. "There were two guns used in the robbery. The clerk was shot with a three fifty-seven Magnum. The bystanders were shot with a thirty-two-caliber revolver. This morning, the police in Mobile matched up our bullet with the bullet taken from the body of the witness in the gas station robbery. Needless to say, the police are very interested to know where we got it."

"What did you say?"

Dan smiled. "I told them the chief of police would give them a full report."

Chief Harper grimaced. "Thanks a lot."

CHAPTER 28

Becky Baldwin nibbled on a french fry.

"How can you eat french fries?" Cora said irritably.

"What? It's heartless under the situation?"

"No, it's unfair to eat fried foods and have a figure like that. If I ate french fries, I'd be big as a house."

"You *are* eating french fries."

"I rest my case."

"What are you so cranky about? You just solved the mystery. You know the secret of Overmeyer's gun."

"How do you figure that?"

"Are you kidding? The gun was involved in a shooting. Overmeyer was a robber. He had a partner in crime. His partner was afraid he was about to come clean, so he killed him."

"Yes, wouldn't that be nice," Cora said.

"What's wrong with it?"

"Just about everything. I spent the morning Googling Overmeyer. Which isn't nearly as dirty as it sounds. You know what type of records they kept in 1954?"

"None?"

"That's right. If the son of a bitch had died, I might have been able to find him. But that would have defeated the whole purpose." Cora frowned. "Uh-oh."

"What?"

"That's Bozo."

"Who?"

"One of Overmeyer's heirs. I bet he's looking for you."

"Big deal. No one knows I'm here."

Cora and Becky were having lunch at the Wicker Basket. A popular home-style restaurant right in the middle of town, it did a brisk lunchtime business.

"Even so, I bet he is."

"Don't be silly," Becky said. "He's probably just here for lunch."

Cruella de Vil stepped out from behind Bozo, pointed a finger.

"Ms. Baldwin?" Bozo said, swooping down on their table. "Ms. Rebecca Baldwin, attorney-at-law?"

Becky smiled. "I'm actually an attorney at lunch."

"Are you the attorney for the Overmeyer estate?"

"Now, there you are inquiring into matters that are best discussed in a law office."

"I'm not asking you to discuss the estate. I'm just asking if you're handling it."

"Come by my office."

"There's no reason to come by your office if you're not handling it."

Cora stuck her nose in. "You see this food here? There's no reason to come by our table if you're not handling it."

"I'm not talking to you."

"You're not talking to me, either," Becky said. She looked at her watch. "Two o'clock. In my office."

"That's going to be a little awkward," Cora said as Bozo and Cruella slunk off.

"What?"

"Explaining you're not the attorney for the estate."

"It may be awkward for them. Not for me."

"How are you going to explain that you made an inventory?"

"I'll refer them to you."

"Thanks a heap."

"So, go on," Becky said. "What's the deal with this robbery? Which I would assume these jokers know nothing about."

"I wouldn't go that far. But Chief Harper

hasn't leaked it yet, if that's what you mean."

"Yeah. So what's the deal? Overmeyer's one of the robbers. His partner's the other. If Overmeyer's about to come clean, his partner's the logical suspect."

"Yeah."

"What's wrong with that?"

Cora shook her head. "It's like I said. If Overmeyer died, there'd be a record. The guy Overmeyer used to pal around with is Rudy Clemson. Korean War buddy. Guy from his platoon."

"Why do I get the feeling I'm not going to like this?"

"The war wasn't over when they went home. Overmeyer took a round in the shoulder. Rudy had a head wound and shrapnel in his hip."

"You making a case for post-traumatic stress?"

"Relax. You don't have to defend these guys in court. They're both dead."

"What?"

"Like I said, the only way we'd have a record of Overmeyer is if he died. Well, same thing with Rudy What's-his-face. Guy kicked the bucket just last year."

"You're kidding."

"Not according to the *Macon County News*

Leader. If Overmeyer had a change of heart late in life and decided to come clean, there's no reason for anyone to want to stop him."

"Too bad," Becky said. "Otherwise, he'd be just the age of the gentleman peering at us through the window."

"Where?"

"Behind you."

"I don't want to turn around. Is he a little guy with his pants up to his armpits?"

"That's him."

"That's the Geezer. Another heir I don't know the name of. But you're right, he's just the age to be his partner if he didn't happen to be dead." Cora frowned. "I suppose that's a careless use of pronouns."

"Wait a minute. How do we know the guy who died was Overmeyer's partner?"

"Good point. We don't. At least, not for sure. But in the next twenty-four hours Dan Finley's about to learn a lot more about Mobile, Alabama."

The Geezer came in the front door, approached the table. "You look like Becky Baldwin."

Cora cocked her head. "She does, doesn't she? I think it's the way the light plays off her hair."

"You're Overmeyer's attorney."

"There even seems to be some dispute about that," Cora said.

"I ain't interested in semantics. No offense meant. I know you're that puzzle person."

"How politically correct of you."

"I understand you've been out to the cabin."

"How do you understand that?" Cora said.

The Geezer made a face. "Why is it I speak to her and you answer?"

"That is unusual, isn't it?" Cora said. "Usually, a lawyer speaks for you. Here I am, speaking for a lawyer."

"Yeah, well, let the lawyer speak for herself. Come on, missy. Was you out there or not?"

"What's your interest in the matter?"

"I'm Herbert's cousin on his mother's side. If you made an inventory, I'd like to know what you found."

"You fixing to inherit?"

"Yeah. But not like them other ones, looking for cash. Grave robbers, that's what they are. Rush in here, lookin' for loot, find out he's been killed. Serve 'em right."

"You're different from them how?" Cora said.

"Ain't lookin' for money. Lookin' for

things with sentimental value. Like the glove."

"What glove?"

"Used to play catch. Out in the backyard. Herbert had a Rawlings glove. All beat up. Ain't worth a damn."

"You think one of the others would try to ace you out of it?" Cora said.

"Just 'cause it's worthless don't mean some idiot don't wanna have it. Get some piece of junk ain't worth a darn, sell it on eBay. If the glove ain't mentioned in the will, they'll be fightin' over it. Glove mentioned in the will?"

"I'm not in a position to comment on that."

The Geezer nodded. " 'Course not. 'Cause that'd be useful. Did you happen to see the glove when you was takin' inventory? Surely you can tell me that."

Becky sighed. "I'm not in a position to confirm or deny."

"Why not? You either saw it or you didn't."

"I can't set that precedent."

"You can't what?"

"If I tell you if there's a glove, some other heir's gonna ask me if I found a safe."

"Didja?"

"See? If I tell you I *didn't* see a glove, they'll say, 'Well, you told him there's no

glove, how come you can't tell me there's
no safe?' And when I don't answer, they'll
take that to mean there's a safe."

"You're telling me there's no glove but
there's a safe?"

"No. I'm telling you that's what people
will think."

"When's the will gonna be read?"

"I have no idea."

"Then there's a will?"

"I didn't say that."

"You said you don't know when it's gonna
be read."

"I don't. That means that in the *event* the
will should exist, I don't know *when* it will
be read."

"You sure sound like an attorney. Even if
you don't look like one."

Harmon Overmeyer swooped down on the
table. "I knew it! I heard there were heirs in
town. You're one of them. You're here for
the money. If any. It's going to be very funny
when they saw up the cabin and split it six
ways."

"And who are you?"

"I'm Harmon Overmeyer. The closest
heir. The *only* heir, as far as I'm concerned.
And I'll be taking a close look at some of
these extremely tenuous claims."

"Well, you go right ahead and look," the

Geezer said. "I'm not making any claims, except what's rightfully mine. If you plan to screw me out of it, I'll be lookin' closely at you. How come you know so much about the estate? You been out there?"

"Not yet."

"Well, you ain't goin', neither. Not till probate says you can. You ain't beatin' me out of anything."

"You have no right to anything."

"Well, you ain't gettin' your greedy mitts on anything that's mine."

"Oh, is that so? I warned the policeman, now I'm warning the lawyer. I don't want these guys near the place, you hear? Not before me. Or there's gonna be hell to pay."

Harmon Overmeyer turned on his heel and stalked off.

"Rather upset, isn't he?" The Geezer grinned fiendishly and trotted after him.

"Well, that spoiled our lunch," Cora said.

"No kidding. Wanna tell Chief Harper?"

"Tell him what? That these guys don't like each other? That's hardly news."

"What if they kill each other?"

Cora grinned. "Go ahead. Make my day."

CHAPTER 29

Cora got home to find Brenda Wallenstein waiting in the driveway. As Sherry's best friend at college, Brenda had always been what the boys called "pleasingly plump." Since marrying Sherry's ex-husband, Brenda had put on a few extra pounds. Cora usually celebrated springing the trap by splurging on extra dessert, but there was such a thing as overdoing it. Brenda's free-flowing smock unfavorably echoed an opera singer.

Cora forced a smile. "Hello, Brenda. What are you doing here?"

"As if you didn't know."

"Excuse me?"

"I'm sorry. I didn't mean that like it sounds. I know it's his fault. It is his fault, isn't it? I'm not just paranoid? Dennis has been around?"

"He passed through town, Brenda. Not that it matters. Sherry isn't here."

"Exactly. So what's he doing?"

Cora sighed. "Brenda, I know you don't want to hear this, but the man you chose to marry is seriously disturbed."

"Stop it! That's the easy answer. That's the answer for everything. Dismiss his actions on the grounds they're not rational."

"Did it occur to you maybe he was checking in with his lawyer?"

"He doesn't have to check in with his lawyer. She made that very clear. Calling her now and then would be quite sufficient."

Buddy had heard their voices and was scratching at the front door.

"I've got to let the dog out. You wanna come in?"

Brenda hesitated a minute, followed Cora up the walk to the front door. The toy poodle shot out, whirled around three times, and circled the yard, peeing on everything.

"My sentiments exactly." Cora held open the door, ushered Brenda in. "Come in. Sit down. Sherry's not here, so no one's cooking, so I got nothing to offer you. Unless you want some milk left over from Reagan's second term."

"I'll pass." Brenda flopped into a chair, popped back up again. "I'm too nervous to sit. Dennis is up to his old tricks. Now he says there's been a murder."

"There *has* been a murder."

"So what? I didn't do it. You didn't do it. It's got nothing to do with him."

"Hey, I'm on your side. Dennis should butt out."

"Then why'd you tell Chief Harper he knows something?"

"Huh?"

"Dennis says you think he knows something about the murder so you told Chief Harper to get it out of him, and the chief won't let him leave town until he tells. But since he doesn't know anything, he can't do that, so he can't leave town."

Cora invoked an amorous act.

"Exactly," Brenda said. "So how much of that is actually your fault?"

"I'd like to lay off some of it on his lawyer. But I suppose I've got to take the hit."

"That's what I thought. So, can you fix it? Can you convince Chief Harper Dennis is lying when he says he knows something?"

"Dennis doesn't say he knows something."

"Huh?"

"To Chief Harper, Dennis claims he doesn't know anything."

"He's lying."

"When?"

"Oh. Good point. Is he lying to you when he says he knows something, or lying to Chief Harper when he says he doesn't?"

"As long as he maintains that position, there's not much I can do."

Brenda looked at Cora for a moment. Her eyes twinkled. "I find that hard to believe."

Cora smiled. "I meant legally."

"I'm sure you did. But if Chief Harper weren't insisting Dennis stick around, you think you could persuade him to leave?"

Cora cocked her head.

"It would be my pleasure."

CHAPTER 30

Dennis Pride scrunched down in the front seat of his rental car and peered over the dashboard with binoculars. He could see the roof of Overmeyer's cabin through the trees. No one was around. He had been watching the cabin for two hours and no one had come near.

There was a car in the driveway next door. The owner was home. Brooks, according to the mailbox. The view from the Brooks house to the Overmeyer cabin was unobstructed. Anyone trying to search the place ran a good chance of being seen.

As Dennis watched, Mr. Brooks came out on the porch. He skipped down the steps, got into the car. It was a Lexus. That figured. Brooks was ten or fifteen years older than Dennis. Not old enough to be old in any negative sense, just old enough to be superior. And here he was owning a nice spread in Connecticut. And without marrying the boss's daughter to do it. At least as far as Dennis knew.

Brooks was going to work late on a week-day, wasn't a nine-to-fiver, clearly had his own cash.

Dennis resented the hell out of him.

Brooks came out of the driveway, hung a left, headed his Lexus back toward town.

As soon as Brooks was gone, Dennis started his car, drove down the road toward the cabin. He went right on by, pulled into Brooks's driveway. He got out, went up on the porch, knocked on the door. He waited a minute, knocked again.

The door was flung open by a woman in her nightgown. At second glance, it was a rather sheer nightgown. And the woman clearly had nothing on under it. If she was aware she was making a spectacle of herself, she didn't let on. She was an attractive young woman, and her eyes were bright. She smiled and said, "Yes?"

"Excuse me. It's about your neighbor next door."

"Yes?"

"I understand he died."

"Oh." She nodded solemnly, lowered her voice. "Yes, he did."

"I'd like to ask your husband a few questions. May I come in?"

"My husband's not here."

"Oh. I'm sorry I missed him. Perhaps I could ask you?"

She frowned. "Ask me what?"

"About your neighbor. Mr. Overmeyer."

"Okay."

She stepped aside and ushered Dennis into a perfectly ordinary, modestly furnished, upper- to middle-class living room, not unlike those of most of the clients he called upon in the course of his job for Wallenstein Textiles. The living room pleased Dennis, made him feel one up on Brooks. He sat in an easy chair just as if he were about to open his briefcase and whip out the latest textile samples.

She sat opposite him on the couch. She asked no questions, just waited for him to go ahead.

"Mrs. Brooks, do you know anything about your neighbor?"

"No."

"You know he's dead, don't you?"

"Yes."

"But you don't know anything else?"

"No."

Dennis took a breath. "Mrs. Brooks, the police think Mr. Overmeyer was murdered."

"Yes, I know."

Dennis opened his mouth, closed it again.

"You do?"

"Oh, yes. It was on the news." She pointed to the high-definition TV, in case Dennis wasn't clear what news she meant.

"So, you know he's been killed, you just don't know any details?"

"Details? What details?"

Dennis felt like a man drowning. Something wasn't right. He didn't want to spook the woman, but he didn't want to let her get away with not answering, either. Was she being deliberately vague and obtuse, or was she just oblivious, like she seemed to be to her attire? Or lack of it. "Yes. Details. Like when he was killed. Or how. Or who did it."

"Probably the man."

Dennis blinked. "Man? What man?"

"The man in the cabin."

"Mr. Overmeyer's cabin?"

"Yes."

"What man was that?"

"The man in the cabin," she explained.

"There was a man in the cabin with Mr. Overmeyer?"

"Yes."

"When?"

"When what?"

"When was the man in the cabin?"

"I don't remember. It was dark. I saw him

in the window. I went out on the porch and looked. It wasn't Mr. Overmeyer. It was a man. He was looking for something."

"How do you know he was looking for something?"

"He climbed on a chair. Stood right up high."

"He climbed on a chair to look on top of something?"

"I couldn't tell what he was looking at. I went to see."

"You went to Mr. Overmeyer's cabin?"

"Yes. I put on my slippers so I wouldn't hurt my feet, and I walked on the grass."

Dennis felt his pulse quicken. "You went to the cabin and saw this man?"

"No. He ran away."

"What?"

"He ran out the door and drove away."

"You saw him leave?"

"Yes."

"What did he look like?"

"It was dark. I couldn't see."

"But you saw him searching the cabin, and you saw him drive off?"

"Yes."

Dennis could have kissed her. Here was his meal ticket. This was information the police didn't have. Information he could barter with Chief Harper to be allowed to stay. What had been just a bluff was legitimate now.

She shook her head in remorse. "I should have stopped him."

"No, you did the right thing," Dennis assured her. "The man was dangerous. He might have hurt you."

"He couldn't hurt me."

"Yes, he could. He probably killed Mr. Overmeyer."

"Yes, but he couldn't hurt me."

Dennis frowned. "Why not?"

She pulled her negligee around her, said calmly, "I have my invisible cloak."

CHAPTER 31

Rick Reed was at his credit-grabbing best. "This is Rick Reed, Channel Eight News, live in Bakerhaven, with an exclusive report. There has been a break in the case of Herbert Overmeyer, the elderly recluse found poisoned in his cabin. So far the police have no leads, but Channel Eight News has come up with one."

The camera pulled back to show Rick standing in a spotlight in front of the Bakerhaven Police Station, and aiming a microphone at a young man in a business suit and long hair. "I am talking to Dennis Pride, who has been assisting the police with their investigation. Mr. Pride, what is it that you have uncovered?"

Dennis was playing it modest. "You understand, I am not a professional investigator. I cannot speak for the police department. However, I have uncovered one small lead."

"What is that?"

"It's possible there is an eyewitness to the crime."

"Why do you say 'possible'?"

Dennis smiled. "Why do you newsmen say 'alleged'? It would appear that there is, but appearances can be wrong."

"Who is this witness?"

"The alleged witness? I couldn't say. But I have every reason to believe a witness exists who can place the killer in Overmeyer's cabin."

"On the night of the murder?"

"Apparently so."

"Why do you say 'apparently'?" The minute the words were out of Rick's mouth, he prayed Dennis wouldn't make another "alleged" crack.

His prayers were answered. "Because the police haven't released the time of the murder yet. Only one of many details the police are not giving out."

"You want to help us with that?"

"The time of the murder?"

"Yes."

"Mr. Overmeyer was likely killed the night before his body was found."

"How do you figure that?"

"Because that is the time at which a witness saw a suspect searching the cabin."

"Searching the cabin? How did the witness know that?"

"The suspect was seen standing on a chair to look on top of a cabinet. If that's not searching, I don't know what is."

"I see," Rick said. Whether he did or not was a toss-up. "So why didn't this witness call the police?"

"He or she didn't want to get involved."

"Why do you say 'he or she'?"

"I don't want to divulge the sex of the witness."

"Do you *know* the sex of the witness?"

"Yes. I just don't want you to know."

"*How* do you know?"

"I can tell." Dennis smiled. "Usually. Our rock band does a cover of Aerosmith's 'Dude (Looks Like a Lady),' but I don't think that's the case here."

Rick Reed blinked, totally lost.

"Anyway, the witness scared the guy off, didn't know Overmeyer was dead, saw no reason to call the police."

"There's a reason now."

"Yes, there is. And I hope the witness will do so."

"*You* didn't call the police?"

"What? Turn someone in? On hearsay evidence? I don't think so. I encouraged the witness to go to the police. I hope the witness does so. In the meantime, I'm going to

185

keep my eyes open."

"If you find anything, bring it to Channel Eight."

Dennis smiled. "You'll be the first to know."

"And there you have it," Rick said. "This is Rick Reed, live in Bakerhaven, with this exclusive, late-breaking news."

Cora choked on her pot pie. Granted, it was frozen in some places, scalding in others — microwaving wasn't her thing — but after what she'd just heard, she probably would have choked on water.

The phone rang. Cora scooped it up. It was Chief Harper. Even over the line she could see the steam coming out of his ears. "Did you see it?"

"You mean Dennis?"

"Good guess."

"Chief —"

"So, you had a great idea. Lean on Dennis and make him tell what he knows. Charge him with obstruction of justice, withholding evidence, and conspiring to conceal a crime. Gee, that couldn't have worked out any better."

"I thought he was bluffing, Chief."

"I thought so, too. I still think so. But now he's bluffing on the goddamn TV."

"What do you want me to do?"

186

"Meet me at the police station."

"Now?"

"I'm calling from my car. Hurry up, before the son of a bitch gets away."

"You want me to help you interrogate him?"

"I want you to stop me from killing him."

CHAPTER 32

Cora fell all over herself getting started. She tried to throw out her pot pie, but the garbage was overflowing. She'd have to dump it, if she just knew where. The hell with it. She tossed the whole thing in the sink, headed for the door.

She realized she'd taken off her tweed skirt. It was hanging on the kitchen chair. She pulled it on, buttoned it. It was tight. Probably why she'd taken it off. What was that all about? Sherry'd been gone a week and a half. Cora was barely eating anything. Just a lot of fast food. And how could it be fattening, if it was fast?

Cora snatched her drawstring purse off the kitchen table, fumbled for a cigarette, and fired one up. Buddy took that as a signal to run in and out of her legs, yipping loudly. She flung some kibble in his bowl, noted that he had water, and darted out the door.

Cora's head was coming off. Keep Chief Harper from killing Dennis? Who was going to keep *her* from killing Dennis? The idiotic, arrogant fool. Mystery witness indeed! Whether he'd actually uncovered one or just made it up was equally bad. Cora wanted to shake him till his teeth rattled and drop him off the roof. There just weren't any buildings in Bakerhaven high enough.

Cora whizzed into town at thirty miles over the speed limit. She was unlikely to be stopped. The town cop was already there. Harper's cruiser was parked in front of the police station. The chief was standing in its headlights. His face was red.

"All right, where the hell is he?" he bellowed.

"Easy, Chief. I don't have him."

"He was right here. Not ten minutes ago."

"Maybe not."

"I saw him myself!"

"Maybe it was on tape."

"He said live. Live from Bakerhaven."

"Yeah, but that's Rick Reed. He was live when he taped it. God knows when that was."

Chief Harper whipped out his cell phone, called information. "This is Chief Harper, Bakerhaven Police. Connect me with Channel Eight News."

Cora's eyes widened. "You can do that?"

"Depends on the operator. Sometimes they argue." He barked into the phone, "This is Chief Harper, get me Rick Reed. . . . I don't care what field he's in, get him on the line. . . . Rick. The interview you did with Dennis Pride. When was that? . . . Oh, yeah, where'd he go after? . . . I'd like a better answer than that. I'm looking for some cooperation here. You help me, I'll help you. . . . How? You got a lot of nerve, asking how. . . . I throw you a lead, now you throw me one."

Harper snapped his cell phone shut. "Country Kitchen."

Cora hopped in her car, followed Chief Harper to the restaurant. It was all she could do to keep up. When she pulled into the parking lot, the chief was already striding up to the door.

It was eleven-thirty. The dining room was nearly empty, but the bar was full.

Dennis Pride was the center of attention. People were gathered around and had apparently been buying him drinks. He was pontificating with the expansive gestures of someone half in the bag. It brought Cora up short to be confronted with such a drunk and realize she had once looked like that. Well, not exactly like that. Or she wouldn't have snared — how many husbands was it now? Depended how you counted. Surely not that annulment.

Harper parted the throng, grabbed Dennis Pride by the lapels, and jerked him off his bar stool. He made a sound like a skydiving water buffalo, flailed his arms to keep his balance. His feet caught up with his head in a rapid series of tiny tiptoe steps.

"All right," Harper said. "So, you're cooperating with the police, are you?"

Dennis focused, recognized the chief. "Yes, I am. I certainly am."

"Good. Cooperating means you got something, you bring it to me. You don't spill it on television."

Dennis was too drunk to take that as a rebuke. Instead, he threw his arm around the chief's shoulders. "That's right. We're a *team.*"

"Right. So who's the witness?"

"Oh. I can't tell you that. That would be violating a trust." Dennis stumbled over the word *violating,* still managed a steely, resolute gaze.

Chief Harper slammed him up against the wall. The air shot out of him, his stomach heaved, and for a second Cora thought he was going to throw up. He gasped for breath, swayed on his feet. If Harper hadn't been holding him, he would have slumped to the floor.

Harper spun him around, handcuffed his hands behind his back. He spun him around again, leaned him against the wall. "You have the right to remain silent. You have the right to an attorney. When she gets here, she's gonna tell you that a conviction of any kind will violate your probation and send you back to serve out your sentence."

Dennis blinked, stared. "Huh?"

Harper yanked him out the door, dragged him down the front steps, slammed him up against the door of his car.

"Hey," Dennis mumbled. "What the hell are you doing?"

Harper raised his fist.

Cora stepped in front of the chief, grabbed Dennis by the chin. "You need a translator, moron? We're going to see your witness, or we're going to jail. Your call."

CHAPTER 33

There was a light on in the Brooks house, but the car was gone.

"They're not here," Harper growled.

Dennis, who'd sobered up some at the threat of jail, said, "He's in the city. She's home."

"She better be." Harper jerked Dennis out of the car.

Cora screeched to a stop behind the cruiser. "Where are they?" she demanded.

"Hubby's out. She's home."

"Says who?"

"Says him."

"Wonderful," Cora said sarcastically. "You can take that to the bank."

Dennis stumbled on the front steps, couldn't put his arms out to break his fall. Harper pulled him to his feet. "Can't you take these off?"

"Show me the witness."

"We're *here*."

"I didn't say show me the *house.*"

Harper rang the doorbell. There was no answer. He rang again. Waited. Pounded on the door.

Headlights came up the driveway. A car door slammed.

George Brooks got out. He wore a suit. His shirt was open at the neck, and his tie was off. He scowled at the people on the porch. "What are you doing here?"

"Mr. Brooks?"

"Yes?"

"Chief Harper. Bakerhaven Police."

"I know who you are. My neighbor's dead. You talked to me before."

"We have some questions for your wife."

"Juliet is not well. You have questions, you can ask me."

"That would not be satisfactory."

"Well, that's how it's going to be."

Cora pushed forward. "Fine, Mr. Brooks. We'll ask you. Did you happen to see anyone in Mr. Overmeyer's cabin the night he was murdered?"

Brooks frowned. "What?"

"It's a simple question. Either you did or you didn't."

"I have no idea what you're talking about."

Cora nodded. "Yeah. That's why we have to ask your wife."

"My wife knows nothing about it."

"She told him she does."

Cora pointed at Dennis. Unfortunately, he had chosen that moment to relapse into the mindless grin of the hopelessly inebriated.

"*He* spoke to my wife?" Brooks said incredulously.

"He was sober at the time," Cora explained. "At least, relatively."

"Mr. Brooks," Chief Harper said, "I don't mean to cause you any trouble, but this is a murder case. Your wife is apparently a witness. I'm sorry if her health is frail, but I need to talk to her."

"Her health is *not* frail. Her mind is . . . Well, I don't see how she could possibly be a witness."

"She has mental problems?"

"She has problems with perception. She couldn't be a witness. I wouldn't let her. It would be cruel."

"We're not talking about taking the witness stand. We're just talking about telling what she knows."

"I doubt she knows anything useful."

"Would she have told you if she did?" Cora asked.

"That's not the point. She might have said anything, and it might not mean anything. I can't have you disturbing her."

Chief Harper said, "I'm sorry, but we have to insist."

Brooks bit his lip. "You're not all going in. You'll scare her, and you won't get anything out of her."

"Okay, just me," Harper said.

Brooks shook his head. "No." He pointed at Cora. "Just her."

"She's not a policewoman."

"No, but she's a woman. She won't scare her." He looked at Cora. "Will you?"

"Of course not," Cora said. "Come on. Let's go."

"This is most irregular," Harper said.

"It certainly is," Cora told him. "See if you can handle your drunk and disorderly. I'll take it from here."

Brooks unlocked the front door, ushered Cora in.

"Honey," he called.

There was no answer.

"She's probably gone to bed."

"She doesn't wait up for you to come home?"

"Sometimes she does, sometimes she doesn't. If she's asleep, we're not waking her."

Cora grunted noncommittally. If Mrs. Brooks was asleep, Cora was using the bed

196

as a trampoline until Sleeping Beauty bounced out of it.

"Where's the bedroom?"

"Upstairs."

Brooks led Cora up a long wooden stairway. On the landing above, he stopped in front of the bedroom door.

"Now then," he warned, "if she's asleep . . ."

Mrs. Brooks was not asleep. She was lying on her back with her head lolled over the edge of the bed at a grotesque angle.

Her throat had been cut.

CHAPTER 34

Cora tackled Brooks, pushed him back toward the door. "Don't touch anything! You can't help her! Get out of here! Now! Or I'll push you down the stairs!"

In a daze, Brooks allowed himself to be led out the front door.

On the porch, Harper was riding herd over Dennis, who had passed out in a lawn chair.

"It's a crime scene!" Cora said. "Call Barney!"

"What?"

"She's dead in the upstairs bedroom. It's a homicide. Her throat's cut. Call your men. I'll hold off the grieving husband and the criminally negligent drunk."

Harper turned to glare at Dennis. "Try not to kill him before I get back."

"It may be hard. Go."

Harper hurried to his car.

Cora whirled around, slapped Dennis across the face.

He moaned, opened his eyes.

She slapped him again.

He jerked away. "Hey!"

Cora glanced over her shoulder.

Brooks had collapsed into a porch chair, his head in his hands.

She pulled Dennis toward her, leaned into his face, lowered her voice. "All right, wise guy. You got a woman killed. When her husband finds out, he's going to beat you senseless. That's him right there. So keep your voice down, tell me what I want to know, or I'm going to tell him who you are."

Dennis Pride was suffering one of the worst blackout drunks of his life. He blinked, uncomprehending, trying to clear the cobwebs. "Huh?"

Cora slapped him across the face. "The right answer is yes. Are you gonna cooperate?"

"I don't know what —"

Cora slapped him again. His eyes teared. "Are you going to cooperate?"

"Yes."

"Good. Your mystery witness. The one you bragged about on TV. What did she tell you?"

"She saw the killer."

"What did he look like?"

"Don't know."

"*You* don't know, or *she* didn't know?"

"Huh?"

Cora slapped him again.

Chief Harper came up the steps. "Hey! What are you doing?"

"Dennis claims Mrs. Brooks saw the killer, but he can't describe him."

"The killer is a him?"

"We don't even know that, do we, Dennis?"

"Huh?"

Cora raised her hand.

Chief Harper grabbed her wrist. "Easy. I'll take it from here. Dennis, what did the woman tell you?"

Dennis blinked. His eyes glazed over.

Harper threw him back in the chair with disgust. "I gotta see the crime scene. Stay here. Don't question him. Or the husband. Make sure no one leaves. Don't let anyone upstairs except Barney and my boys."

Harper went inside before Cora could protest.

A police car pulled up and Sam Brogan got out. Bakerhaven's crankiest officer must have been patrolling nearby to have gotten there so fast. He stroked his mustache, popped his gum.

"What have we got?"

"It's a homicide. The chief's upstairs at

the crime scene."

He jerked his thumb at Brooks. "That the perp?"

"That's the husband."

Sam's shrug was eloquent. "Is that a yes?"

"Sam."

Sam gave Brooks a look and went in.

Cora sighed and sat down to wait for the others.

Dan Finley beat Barney Nathan by a car length. No doubt the doctor would have been first had he not stopped to tie his bow tie. Cora couldn't remember ever seeing him without it.

"Where's the chief?" Dan Finley asked.

Cora sprang up to head him off. "He's upstairs. He wants you to secure the crime scene, make sure no one gets in and these two don't leave. You got crime scene tape?"

"In the car."

"Get it. I'll take the doc upstairs."

Cora hustled Barney Nathan up to the bedroom, where Sam Brogan was already snapping photos.

Harper rose from the body. "Pronounce her, Barney, so we can get on with it."

"She's dead. Go to it."

"Aren't you going to examine her?"

"Her throat's cut. You can't live with your throat cut. I could have pronounced her on the phone."

"Doc," Harper warned, rolling his eyes toward Cora.

Barney waved it away. "You're not going to give me trouble over that, are you, Cora? I'm sure you'll find something much worse."

"You want to give me a time of death, Barney?"

"Now that's the type of thing she'll nail me on. Well, it's gotta be within the last couple of hours. I'll pin it down with the body temperature when I get her back to the morgue."

Cora said, "You wouldn't say it was within the last half hour?"

Barney frowned. "Why?"

Harper said, "You happen to see the evening news?"

"Oh." Barney looked at his watch. Frowned. "That would be cutting it thin. That's what you mean, right? That she was killed because of the broadcast."

"It's a nonmedical factor, Barney. Don't let it influence you." Harper frowned. "Where the hell is Dan? I called him the same time I called you." It dawned on him that Cora was in the room. "What are you doing here? You're supposed to be watching Dennis."

"Dan is. He's stringing the crime scene

ribbon. To keep the media out."

"Media? What media?" Harper's face darkened. "Go down there, send Dan up. If he tipped off Rick Reed, he'll wish he hadn't. The son of a bitch helped kill this woman. Go on. Get."

Cora reluctantly went back downstairs. Dan Finley had strung the crime scene ribbon and was up on the porch.

"You didn't call Rick Reed, did you?" Cora asked.

"Why? Because of the interview? He didn't mention her by name."

"No, but the killer'd know who he was talking about."

"It's not Rick's fault. He's just doing his job."

"Maybe so, but don't call him."

"That from you?"

"That's from the chief. He's not happy, and there's no reason to make it worse. Go upstairs, I'll hold things down here."

Headlights turned off the main road, and the Channel Eight News van bumped up the drive.

"Dan," Cora said.

Dan looked defensive. "Well, you could have told me sooner."

Rick Reed exploded from the van, dashed up on the porch. "Is this it? Where is she?"

Dan grinned sheepishly.

Cora raised a finger. "Easy, Rick."

"Easy, hell. Is it a murder or not? Where's Chief Harper?"

"I don't think you want to be interviewing the chief just now."

"Why not?"

Cora grimaced. "Rick, you're one of the dumbest people I ever met, and I married some pretty dumb ones. Your little interview with Dennis here probably *caused* the killing. How do you think the chief feels about that?"

"Oh, come on. I'm not responsible for what people do." Rick glanced over his shoulder. "You wanna hurry up with that camera?"

The news crew, struggling with the heavy equipment, didn't look thrilled to be prompted.

"Wanna give me a statement?" Rick asked Cora.

"I do, but you couldn't use it on the air."

"How about you, Dan?"

"Not a chance."

Rick jerked his thumb at Dennis. "Can you wake him up?"

"No."

Rick smiled. "Don't be like that. We're all in this together. Who's this guy?"

"Leave him alone," Cora said.

"Who is he?"

"George Brooks. The husband."

"That'll do."

The crew aimed the camera, snapped on the lights.

"I wouldn't advise it," Cora said. "The guy's not going to take too kindly to you."

"Just doing my job." Rick cleared his throat. "This is Rick Reed, Channel Eight News, live from Bakerhaven, where tonight this peaceful town was rocked by a savage crime, the murder of — Hell! Cut! What's her name?"

"Mrs. Brooks."

"First name?"

"Don't know."

Rick glanced dubiously at the husband, decided to let it go. "Okay, take it again. This is Rick Reed, Channel Eight News, coming to you live —"

Before Rick could finish, George Brooks stood up, grabbed him by the shoulder, spun him around, and punched him in the mouth.

CHAPTER 35

Chief Harper wrestled George Brooks into the kitchen. Rick Reed had roused the husband from his funk. After being nearly catatonic, the man was livid.

"Son of a bitch!"

"Easy," Harper said. "Easy."

"My wife is dead! And then I hear it's his fault!"

"It's not his fault."

"Oh, no? What's this about an interview?"

"He's a reporter. They interview people. Sometimes they're irresponsible."

"Irresponsible!"

Cora peered over Chief Harper's shoulder. "Someone killed your wife. That's who you're really angry at."

"I don't need your amateur psychology!"

"But you need to calm down." With Chief Harper's help, Cora managed to guide Brooks into a seat at the kitchen table. "Look here. Whoever did this will not get away with it. I promise you that."

Brooks blinked.

Cora Felton was decked out in her finest Miss Marple attire, a white blouse and tweed skirt, and she looked as she did in the picture that adorned her Puzzle Lady column, like everyone's favorite grandmother.

"*You* promise me?"

"I'm tougher than I look, buster. We're gonna get this guy, but we're gonna need your help. You need to calm down, answer Chief Harper's questions, help him do his job."

Brooks glared at her a moment. Then his lip trembled, and he heaved a huge sigh. "I can't believe it. I simply can't believe it."

"Easy," Chief Harper said. "I know this is hard, but we have to do it. You think you can answer questions?"

"Yeah."

"You were gone all day?"

"I was in New York City."

"On business?"

"I work in New York."

"What do you do?"

"I work for an insurance company. What difference does it make? How could this happen?"

"What did you do after work?"

"I went out with the guys."

"Guys from the office?"

"That's right."

"Where'd you go?"

"Huh? Oh, have some drinks. Shoot some pool."

"You didn't get home until eleven-thirty?"

"That's not late."

"You got to the house and found us here?"

"That's right."

"And then you went upstairs. With no idea what you would find?"

"Of course not."

"Your wife was home alone?"

"Yes."

"She was in her nightgown. What time does she go to bed?"

"When she gets tired."

"Eleven-thirty wasn't early for her to go to bed?"

"No. What are you getting at?"

"Just trying to get the general picture. When was the last time you saw your wife alive?"

He shuddered at the question. "When I left for work this morning."

Cora leaned in. "Did you speak to her during the day?"

He frowned. "Why do you ask?"

"I'm just wondering if you did."

"I called her to say I'd be late."

"When was that?"

"In the afternoon. I don't remember what time."

"Before you went out with the boys?" Cora said.

"Yes. That's right."

"Hmm."

Brooks looked at her.

Harper jumped back in. "Does your wife work?"

"No, she doesn't."

"She was home all day?"

"Yes."

"Alone?"

Brooks moaned slightly. "I didn't think."

"Of course not. How could you?"

"Well, the Overmeyer murder might have been a hint," Cora said dryly.

Brooks glared. So did Chief Harper. Neither man could quite believe she'd said that.

"Sorry," Cora said. "But we're tiptoeing around the subject here. Which can only make it worse. Mr. Brooks, can you think of anyone who'd want to harm your wife?"

"Juliet? No. Of course not."

"Do you think it's true? What Dennis said? Do you think she did see someone in Overmeyer's cabin that night?"

Brooks's shoulders heaved. His anger gave way to despair. He looked completely overwhelmed.

"I have no idea."

CHAPTER 36

Chief Harper sipped his third cup of coffee, ran his fingers through his thinning hair. "It's a mess. An utter disaster."

"You got the autopsy report?" Cora asked.

"Not yet. Barney says if I call him one more time, he's gonna let the answering machine pick up."

"One good thing. There's no crossword puzzle involved."

"So? If there was a puzzle, at least I'd have a reason for consulting you. As it is, I'm a chief of police taking advice from an amateur detective crossword puzzle columnist for no earthly reason."

"Hey, just because I don't have a license doesn't mean I'm no good."

"I know it and you know it. John Q. Public doesn't know it. Outside of Bakerhaven, I mean."

"Well, you've got a crime to solve, and I'd love to help you do it. We've got a little bit of a breather, because Aaron wasn't here to cover it for the paper, and Brooks cold-cocked Rick Reed."

Harper had to smile at that. The victim's husband had hit the on-camera reporter so hard, he hadn't been able to file a report.

Cora settled into her chair, pulled out her cigarettes.

"Don't even think about it," Harper said.

"I thought you wanted me here."

"Not if you're gonna smoke. If you're gonna smoke, go out and come back."

"Aw, hell." Cora shoved the cigarettes into her purse. "I should warn you, when I have a nicotine fit, I get nasty."

"And we all know what happens then," Harper said dryly. "You start abusing suspects."

"Oh, Dennis is a suspect?"

"Suspect or witness, you can't beat them up."

"He's drunk. He won't even remember."

"Like that makes it better."

"We needed to know what he knew."

"*We?* Leave me out of it. I wasn't up on the porch slapping him around."

"You know what I mean. The woman's dead. We have to know what she knew." Cora looked around. "So, where is he? You got him locked up?"

"I probably should have. For his own good. I left him in a motel on Route Nine. Figured that would keep him out of trouble."

"Unless he wakes up and drives off."

"His car's at the Country Kitchen."

"Good move. Where's hubby? You didn't let him stay home, did you?"

"No. He's in a motel."

"Not the same one?"

"Just as far away as I can get."

"Dennis should have sobered up by now. Wanna send Dan out to bring him in?"

"I was planning to."

"So?"

"After you leave."

"What?"

"Cora, you punched him out. Maybe not as bad as Brooks hit Rick Reed, but if he wakes up with any recollection of what happened, you're in serious trouble."

"You think I couldn't take him sober?"

"Don't be silly. He'll sue you for damages."

"*That* wimp? Give me a break. He wouldn't even think of it."

"Yeah, but he's got a pretty sharp lawyer."

"Becky wouldn't sue me."

"She might not have a choice. He's a client. If it's in his best interests to sue, how's she gonna stop him? It would be malpractice."

"She could always quit."

Harper grimaced. "I'm not sure she's got so many clients she can afford to throw one away."

"All right. I understand. I'm a bad girl, I'm in trouble, I can't afford to prod Dennis with a stick. If I promise not to piss him off, will you let me stay?"

"You think you can keep your promise if he acts like a jerk?"

"If? Come on. We *know* he's gonna act like a jerk. I'll keep quiet and let him do it. Come on. Whaddya say?"

Dan Finley stuck his head in the door.

"Dan," Harper said. "Just who I wanted to see. Wanna run over and pick up Dennis Pride?"

"He's here."

"What?"

"He's out front. With his attorney. Becky Baldwin. He wants to see you."

"Uh-oh."

Cora smiled. "See, Chief? It's not my fault. I just happened to be here."

"I wouldn't be so happy if I were you. He brought his lawyer."

"He's not gonna sue me."

Dan ushered Becky and her client in.

Dennis had washed his face, combed his hair, and tied his tie, but his eyes were red as beets. He looked like a guy nursing a hell of a hangover.

"This is a surprise," Harper said. "I kind of thought you'd stay put. What do you want?"

"First off," Becky said, "he wants his car. You abandoned this man with no means of transportation. That is totally unacceptable. We want that car, and we want it now."

"Take it."

"Where is it?"

"You don't know?"

"No. Where did you put it?"

"I haven't touched it. I assume it's at the Country Kitchen. That's where I picked him up. If he doesn't remember, that's a good indication he shouldn't have been driving."

"Did you charge him with DUI?"

"No, I did not."

"Then that claim has no merit."

Harper shrugged. "You're the one who brought it up. So, are you here as his attorney?"

"Yes, I am."

"Good. I have some questions for Dennis, and I would hope you are going to advise him to answer them."

"We'll get to that," Becky said. "First I

215

have some business."

She flopped a briefcase down on Harper's desk, reached in, took out a paper.

Harper raised his eyebrows, glanced at Cora. "That looks like a summons."

"Yes, it is."

"What's the charge?"

"Aggravated assault."

Cora sucked in her breath.

"Don't say I didn't warn you," Harper told her.

"You're suing me?" Cora said incredulously.

"Of course not." Becky turned to the chief, slapped the summons into his hand. "Chief Harper, you are charged with aggravated assault on my client, Dennis Pride, for illegally and without sufficient grounds taking him into custody last night in the Country Kitchen. I am filing suit for assault and battery, false arrest, using excessive force, and humiliating my client, who is blameless. The incident, I understand, happened in front of dozens of witnesses. We are asking one million dollars actual damages and four million dollars punitive damages."

Becky cocked her head and smiled. "Now then. You have some questions?"

CHAPTER 37

Becky dropped Dennis off at the Country Kitchen. He got in his car, backed up, pulled out of the lot.

Before Becky could follow, Cora drove up behind her, cutting her off.

Cora was out of her car in a flash. "Becky, you can't do this."

"Do what?"

"Sue Chief Harper."

"It was either that or sue you."

"What?"

"Dennis seems to recall being roughed up at the victim's house. Of course, it's only a vague recollection, and there aren't any witnesses. At the Country Kitchen, there's plenty. And it's a much better suit. If I sue you, I have to go into court, prove you beat him up. You're old enough to be his —"

"Watch it!"

"You see my problem? But an authority

figure like a policeman, much more plausible."

Cora's eyes widened. "You're suing Chief Harper because I slapped Dennis around?"

"I'm just stating the situation."

"And you complain about lawyer jokes!"

"Was my client roughed up or what?"

"You don't think he had it coming? Off the record, I mean?"

"Of course," Becky said. "This is *all* off the record, or I wouldn't be talking to you. This conversation is hypothetical and never happened. It *wouldn't* have happened, if you weren't blocking my car."

"Becky. This is not fun and games. Two people are dead."

"I know. And the killer should be brought to justice, yada, yada, yada. That's true. We still gotta play by the rules. I got a client says he was abused. He may not be a model citizen, but most clients aren't. I gotta take it seriously."

Cora waved it away. "Yeah, yeah. Forget all that. What does Dennis know about the murder?"

Becky looked surprised. "Nothing."

"But he talked to the woman. What did she tell him?"

"You know what she told him. Exactly what he said on TV."

"He didn't tell her story on TV."

"Yes, he did. The only thing he withheld was her name."

"That's all he knows?"

"Yes."

"So, why wouldn't you let him talk to Chief Harper?"

"I *did* let him talk to Chief Harper."

"You did all the talking."

"That's what lawyers do."

"Dennis isn't withholding anything?"

"No."

Cora looked Becky in the eyes, shook her head. "You should play cards. I can't tell if you're bluffing. The problem is, you file the damn suit, then you do all the talking for your client. I can't tell if you're being coy about the murder, or just reluctant to discuss the damage suit."

"I don't *know* anything about the murder."

"Maybe not. But your client's been snooping around for days. You know it, I know it. Calling on Mrs. Brooks wasn't the only thing he did. If you find out anything else, give me a heads-up."

"I can't do that."

"You can't let a killer go free, Becky."

"I wouldn't do that."

"How about an accessory to murder?"

"Huh?"

"Your client's interview on TV probably got the woman killed. Let's not lose sight of that."

"It's not a crime."

"Maybe not, but it might be actionable."

"What?"

"What if hubby gets a lawyer? Files a wrongful death suit? How'd you like to be defending that?"

"I suppose I'd get paid for it."

"Come on, Becky. You're too young to be cynical."

"That's not cynical. That's just practical. You wanna let me out of here? I got work to do."

"Does any of it concern me?"

"Not if you play your cards right."

"Was that a threat?"

Becky shrugged. "I don't know. Might be a bluff." At Cora's irritation, she added, "You know, I think I like this poker metaphor."

CHAPTER 38

Chief Harper wasn't in the best of moods. He had a summons for aggravated assault on his desk and a gaggle of Overmeyer heirs outside his door. Cora had to fight her way through them to get into the office. She kicked the door shut, flopped into the chair next to the desk, and said, "How's tricks?"

"Well," Harper said glumly, "according to my insurance carrier, I am covered for claims arising from false arrest. However, there seems to be some question as to whether that applies. They point out I never actually booked Dennis Pride. In light of which, they maintain, this is *not* a false arrest but an aggravated assault. In which case they're not willing to concede that I'm covered." Harper cocked his head. "I'm trying to decide if it's too early to start appraising my house. Becky's only got an apartment, she could probably use a house."

"Chief —"

"Which wouldn't be so galling if *you* weren't the one who beat Dennis up."

"No one's taking your house, Chief. This won't even go to court. If it did, the insurance company would defend it, because people would stop buying their coverage if they didn't. But you know and I know that isn't going to happen. Because Dennis is a huge wimp, and when you file a counter-charge of obstruction of justice, he's going to cave in like that." Cora snapped her fingers. Jerked her thumb at the door. "So what are the happy heirs doing?"

"Alibis."

"Huh?"

"I'm checking their alibis."

"How'd you get 'em in here?"

"They came of their own accord. Wanna know why I won't let 'em leave town."

"They wanna leave town?"

"For the most part. Soon as it turned out we're solving a murder instead of probating a will."

Cora nodded. "That makes sense. What *doesn't* make sense is if they're not interested in inheriting, why would they have done it?"

"I admit, these theories aren't fleshed out."

"How are they doing with alibis?"

"The Westons alibi each other."

"Who's that?"

"The guy with red hair and the skinny woman."

"Oh. Bozo and Cruella."

Harper grimaced. "Please. I have enough trouble without images like that in my head. Anyway, Alan and Ellen Weston claim they were back in their motel watching a movie on TV. Didn't see the evening news. Didn't know there'd been a murder until this morning."

"There are movies on at eleven o'clock?"

"The motel gets free HBO. So they say. I haven't checked up yet, but it would be a stupid claim to make if it wasn't true."

"Hmmm."

"Isn't this where you say, 'I've met some pretty stupid killers in my day'?"

"Yeah, but falsely claiming to have HBO defies stupidity. More likely the motel has HBO, they looked up to see if a movie was playing at that time, and are claiming to have watched it."

"You think they're guilty?"

"Hell, no. I'm just saying their alibi's worthless. They could have watched the eleven o'clock news, heard Dennis blab about the witness, rushed out and killed her, come back, and checked the TV schedule for something they could claim they were watching instead of the evening news. A movie on HBO would fill the bill."

"Think I should get 'em back in here?"

"I don't know what you're gonna prove, unless you wanna grill 'em on the plot of the movie. What movie was it, by the way?"

"*The Sixth Sense.*"

Cora made a face. "Oh, phooey. Everyone's seen *The Sixth Sense.* 'I see dead people. On TV. Not in the bedroom where I'm slitting her throat.' You can count on it they know the plot. They wanna leave, by the way?"

"Just as fast as they can. Which doesn't mean they did it, but doesn't mean they didn't."

"Right," Cora said. "Who else you got?"

"A Mr. Snively stayed at a bed-and-breakfast. He thinks the owners saw him come in."

"That doesn't mean they didn't see him go out. Whose bed-and-breakfast was it?"

"Marge and Bob's."

"The Mercers?" Cora snorted. "Scratch that alibi. Marge is deaf as a post. Bob likes his gin. By eleven o'clock, you'd have your run of the place. What heir was that?"

"Mr. Snively."

"That doesn't help."

"Whiny voice. Three-piece suit."

"Oh, the Cranky Banker. Snively fits him fine. His alibi's no better or worse than Bozo and Cruella's. Who else?"

"Harmon Overmeyer. I'd love to get him on murder, but he's more likely to kill one of the others. Insists that he's the real heir and they're just party crashers. Furious that they're here. He's got no alibi. Staying at a motel alone. Says he didn't watch the evening news. Had a drink and went to bed early. He blames me for the other heirs being here. In a way he's right, because I won't let 'em leave. But I didn't bring 'em. Which is what he's implying. That I attracted 'em. Through reckless statements made by me and Becky Baldwin. Nonsense, of course, but Becky assures me a lawyer can argue anything."

"At least in that case she'd be arguing on your side," Cora said dryly. "What about the Geezer? You got the dope on him?"

"Fred Goldman? Sure. What's *his* nickname?"

"The Geezer."

"Oh. Guess I walked into that one."

"Does he have an alibi?"

"No. And proud of it. At least he gets a kick out of telling me so to my face. He's staying in the same motel as Dennis Pride.

Not that it means anything. Dennis wasn't there at the time of the murder. The Geezer says he was. Points to no corroborating evidence whatsoever. Except . . . Guess what he was doing?"

"What?"

"A crossword puzzle."

"Are you kidding me?"

"Relax. It was one of yours. Nothing in there about crime, was there?"

"How the hell should *I* know?" Cora cried.

Harper looked at her in surprise. "Easy. No one's accusing you of anything. I'm just saying, it's your simple everyday column. You didn't have a column in yesterday's paper relating to crime?"

"I have no *idea* what's in yesterday's paper," Cora said irritably. "These things are written way in advance. By the time they see the light of day, I'm into something else entirely. The guy solved the puzzle. Just ask him to produce it."

"Yeah."

"Yeah what?"

"I'd feel stupid doing it."

"Now you know how *I* feel. You bring me all these crossword puzzles, figure they must have meaning. Some don't. Is that everyone?"

"No. There's Cindy Barrington."

"Who?"

"The girl with too much makeup."

"Oh. The Hooker."

Harper winced. "Do you suppose you could come up with a more suitable nickname?"

"I could, but they'd bleep it."

"Cora."

"She have an alibi?"

"No. Says she was out for a walk."

"At eleven o'clock at night?"

"Exactly."

"Where did she say she was going?"

"Just walking around."

"Around what?"

"She didn't know."

"That's not good."

"No. You'd like a destination. At least a point of reference."

"I wouldn't want to criticize your investigative techniques, Chief, but this is less than helpful."

"No kidding. Think you could do better?"

"I couldn't do any worse. Mind if I ask a few questions?"

"Go ahead."

"Why are they still here?"

"I didn't mean of *me.*"

"I know. I'm going to question them. I'm just curious. What reason did you give them for sticking around?"

"I didn't give them a reason. I just told them to stay."

"And they did?"

"I'm a cop."

"Come again?"

"I questioned them one at a time. When I finished with one, I asked for another. They're out there wondering what comes next."

"What comes next?"

"I have no idea. I was waiting for you to get back."

"That isn't funny."

"Well, I was waiting for something. Actually, I'm waiting for everything. I'm waiting for the autopsy report. I'm waiting for the fingerprints to get processed."

"What fingerprints?"

"The ones that are going to turn out to be Juliet or George Brooks." Harper shook his head. "The big problem here is it's too simple a crime. She saw the killer. The killer found out, thanks to Dennis and Rick Reed, and shut her up."

The phone rang.

Harper scooped it up. "Chief Harper. . . . Hi, Barney, what you got? . . . I know she was killed with a razor. . . . The sole cause of death? Why wouldn't it be? . . . Okay, you're saying she was alive when her throat was cut. She wasn't drugged, or knocked out, or manhandled that you can see. So when did she die?" Harper's face hardened. "Give me that again. . . . You must be mistaken. . . . I don't care what methods you used, I just want to know the time. . . . Well, that can't be right."

Harper slammed the phone down. "Damn!"

"What's the problem?"

"She was killed between nine and ten."

CHAPTER 39

Cora paced up and down the office. "I need a smoke."

"Not in here."

"You need my help."

"Go outside."

"If I go out there, those vultures will tear me apart."

"Chew some gum."

Cora fed a stick of Juicy Fruit into her mouth, continued to pace. "So, what does this mean?"

"In the first place, those alibis are no good."

"They were no good anyway."

"Yeah, but now even at face value they're moot. We need to know where they were between nine and ten."

"Why?"

"What do you mean, why?" Harper said. "That's when the murder took place."

"Yeah, but we just lost the motive. If the

murder happened before the broadcast, the murder wasn't triggered by the broadcast. So the idea it's cause and effect is suspect."

"But it's linked to the Overmeyer murder."

"That's what's suspect."

"Well, what if it *isn't?* Suppose the murder isn't linked to the Overmeyer murder? What then?"

"You got a load of crap," Cora said. "That's the type of thing most likely to make me throw a book across the room. Two people who live next door to each other murdered within a week of each other, but they're separate crimes? That happens in a book, you take the author out and shoot him. You wipe his hard drive and confiscate his mouse. The crimes *must* be related. One way or another, they must."

"No argument here. So, what do we do next?"

"Find out where everyone was between nine and ten."

"You just got through saying that won't help."

"Yeah, but it must. The crimes have to be related, so the suspects are those who prosper. Even without the TV interview."

"And the TV interview is just a co-incidence?"

Cora grimaced. "I hate that, too. But it's the lesser of two evils. The TV interview being a coincidence isn't nearly as bad as the murders being a coincidence."

"You mean you'd let the writer live?"

"Just barely. It's less egregious."

"You and your words."

"What?"

"Egregious."

"Oh." Cora hadn't even noticed she'd used it. Living with Sherry was wearing off on her. That and her newfound expertise with sudoku. Without realizing it, Cora was relaxing into the role of the Puzzle Lady.

Chief Harper opened the door, and Harmon Overmeyer practically fell in.

"Listening at the keyhole?" Cora said.

Harmon flushed. "Not at all. I was just coming to find out when I could go."

"It didn't occur to you to ask earlier?"

Harmon stuck out his chin at Chief Harper. "Why is *she* answering me? You're the sheriff. I'm talking to you."

"I'm actually the chief of police."

"I don't care what you call yourself. The fact is you're in charge. And she isn't. She's not even a policeman."

Cora shrugged. "I keep failing the exam."

"See? She's mocking me. I don't have to

put up with that. You're in charge. Can I leave?"

"You mean leave the police station or leave the jurisdiction?"

"I don't want to leave town. I'm here to inherit the estate. I just don't want to sit out there with those impostors."

"How do you know they're impostors?"

"How do I know anything? I'm his closest relative. You said so. Suddenly there's a whole bunch closer? I don't think so. They're just scavengers circling the kill."

Cora smiled. "You paint a lovely picture of the dear departed."

Chief Harper cut off Harmon's retort. "Children, please. You want to fight, do it on your own time. Right now I have some questions. Where were you last night from nine to ten?"

"Why?"

"It has some bearing on the murder."

"She was killed between nine and ten?"

"I'm not saying that. But I'd like to know where you were."

"You mean I'm a suspect?"

"The more you evade the question, the more you become one," Cora said dryly. "He's got a whole roomful of people to question. How about giving him a break?"

"What's the question?"

"Where were you between nine and ten?"

"Last night? I don't know. I was in a strange town. I didn't know anyone. And I must say the bed-and-breakfast where I'm staying is no help."

"Who's that?" Cora asked.

"The Crowleys."

"Oh."

"What did you do?" Harper prompted.

"I can't remember."

"Were you in your room at the bed-and-breakfast?"

"Between nine and ten? That seems too early. I was probably just getting back from dinner."

"Where did you eat?"

"Someplace out on the road. Looks like a log cabin."

"Oh. The Country Kitchen?"

"That's the place."

"You were there until ten o'clock?"

"I have no idea how long I was there."

"Did you eat alone?"

"I just got here. I don't know anyone."

"So you ate alone?"

"Yes."

"Is there anyone who can corroborate the fact you were in the Country Kitchen?"

"The waitress might remember me."

"Why, you stiff her on the tip?" Cora said. Harmon shot her a look.

"How'd you pay for the meal?" Harper asked.

"Why?"

"If you used a credit card, there'll be a record."

"You're really looking for proof I was in the Country Kitchen last night?"

"Of course he is," Cora said irritably. "It's a murder investigation. If you're not involved, stop being such a horse's ass and give him some help."

"I paid with American Express. I may have the receipt." He fished in his wallet. "Yes, here you go."

Harper took the receipt. "According to this, you paid at nine-fifteen."

"Let me see that." Cora snatched the receipt out of Harper's hands, checked the total. "I apologize for suggesting you stiffed the waitress. You gave her a very generous eight percent."

Harmon grabbed the receipt, stuffed it in his wallet. "So, when do you think there's the slightest chance you'll get to the bottom of this and we can settle the estate?"

"You want to speed things up, you might confess," Cora told him.

Chief Harper marched Harmon out and

came back with Bozo and Cruella, who split on where they were between nine and ten. Bozo thought they were at the B&B. Cruella thought they were in the mall.

"Most mall stores close at nine," Cora pointed out.

"Not all of them. The Wal-Mart's open later. In fact, that's how I know it was between nine and ten. The other stores were closed."

"That's easy enough to verify," Harper said.

"Verify? We had nothing to do with this. We weren't even around. We just wanna go home."

"You don't care about the estate?" Cora said.

"We've seen the estate. Split six ways it hardly pays us bus fare."

The Geezer had no alibi, either.

"Nine to ten? I thought it was eleven to twelve. Or is this something else?"

"No, it's the same thing."

The Geezer sucked something from between his teeth. "Then I can't help you. I didn't kill her between eleven and twelve, and I didn't kill her between nine and ten neither."

"You know where you were at the time?"

"At the time I did. You ask me then, I

could have told you."

Chief Harper's headache was getting worse. "Do you *remember* where you were at the time?"

"Let's see. This is last night. This is a couple of hours before you asked me before. That's between nine and ten." He cocked his head, furrowed his brow. "I was either at the motel or I wasn't."

"Where would you be if you weren't at the motel?"

"You got me."

"Where'd you have dinner?" Cora asked.

He had to think a minute. "Drive-through." He jerked his thumb. "Back toward town."

Cora figured by "town" he meant New York. "The McDonald's?"

"Or the other one."

"Burger King?"

"Whatever. Look, you wanna go ahead and solve this thing so I can get my inheritance?"

"That may take some time," Harper told him.

"Is that right. Well, would the police department like to pick up my motel bill while I'm waitin'?"

"Sorry," Harper said.

"I'll bet you are." Geezer cocked his head.

"So, with all the excitement, I don't suppose you done nothin' 'bout finding the will?"

"No will has turned up yet."

"Turned up. There's a phrase. Kinda indicative of the whole investigation."

Harper took a breath. "I assure you, the Overmeyer case is being thoroughly investigated."

"You mean you searched the place and you can't find a will."

"We searched the place. We haven't found a will. That doesn't mean we're done looking. It's possible Overmeyer had a bank account or safe-deposit box. It's possible he had a lawyer draw a will. The only attorney in town didn't do it, but some other lawyer may come forward."

"You better hope so," Cora said. "If he died intestate, it's going to be a mess."

"What'll happen?"

Cora shrugged. "Seeing as how none of you were particularly close relatives, I imagine a judge would proportion it equally. Of course, what that means is anybody's guess. Do you count the couple as one heir or two? You'd think one, because the other married into it. But with relationships as tenuous as these, there's always a married-into-it in the equation."

"That's all well and good. The point is whatever I got comin', I want it."

"No one's trying to gyp you out of it," Cora said. "On the other hand, if there's no will, it may be months before it goes through probate."

"Months?!" the Geezer erupted. "Well, that's a fine howdy do! You expect me to wait months for what's mine?"

"Why did you do that?" Harper said, closing the door on the Geezer.

"Just prodding him to see how much he cared. Apparently, it's quite a bit."

"Is that right about the probate taking months?"

"How should I know? I never killed a husband. Wanted to, never did. Always divorced them. So I've never been through probate. Now, alimony and property settlements, I'm a whiz."

"Do me a favor," Harper said.

"What's that?"

"Don't prod the next one."

Next up was the Hooker, who looked as if she'd gotten caught in a police sting. Her makeup was more garish than usual, the lipstick smeared, the rouge blotchy, the mascara caked with tears.

"It's not my fault," she said, sniffling. "I had nothing to do with it, I don't care about the money anymore, I just want to go home."

"You don't care about the money?" Cora said.

"No. I'd kiss it off right now if you'd let me leave."

"That's an unusual attitude," Harper said. "Most heirs want to inherit."

"Inherit what? A musty old cabin full of junk. No bank account. No liquid assets. Nothing to split. Now people are dying and you want to know where we were between nine and ten."

Cora said, "That's very interest—"

Chief Harper cut her off. "Yes, it is. Miss . . ." He nearly called her Hooker, fumbled with the paper to find her name.

Cora seized the opportunity to jump back in. "I got a question here, Chief."

"I'm sure you do. I got a question of my own. Miss Barrington, I asked you about the time between eleven and twelve. How did you know I was interested in the time between nine and ten?"

Cora suppressed a groan.

"Are you kidding? Everyone's talking about it. Isn't that what you asked the others?"

Harper smiled ruefully.

"That's the problem with leaving wit-

240

nesses in the outer office," Cora said. "You're better off locking them up."

The Hooker looked concerned.

"She's joking," Harper said. "So people are talking about it. What are they saying?"

"They're saying you don't seem to know any more about it than they do, but it must have taken place between nine and ten because that's what you're asking."

"So," Harper said. "Then you've had time to figure out where you were."

"Yes. I was in my motel room wishing I'd never heard of this damn town."

"How *did* you hear of it?" Cora put in.

"Huh?"

"How did you hear your dear — What was he to you?"

"Great-uncle."

"How did you hear your dear great-uncle had gone to the land of probate?"

"Oh."

"Hadn't thought of that one?"

"I forget who told me. I got a phone call."

"From a relative?"

"No."

"I didn't think so. If it was a relative, they'd be here. So who was it?"

"Just a friend. Who'd seen an obituary, or death notice, or something. Just called to see if I was related, and, of course, I am."

"How'd you know?"

"Huh?"

"You obviously weren't close. Did you even know you *had* a great-uncle? How'd you know he was a relative?"

"I looked it up on the Internet."

Cora nodded. "Of course."

CHAPTER 40

Cora came out of the police station and walked across the street to the Bakerhaven Town Library.

Edith Potter was at the front desk. The librarian had her hair done, the gray touched up with auburn highlights. Cora had to admit, she looked good. Cora never dyed her hair, at least not since she made a play for that amazingly rich oil man who liked them young. The hair had been insufficient, as Cora learned ruefully when the gentleman in question ultimately hooked up with a sweet young thing who probably still watched *Sesame Street*.

Cora and Edith exchanged the usual tut-tuts about the murders.

"Jimmy around?" Cora asked.

"Yes, he is. You need some help?"

"Would he mind?"

"He'd be delighted."

Edith's son Jimmy was back from community college, which was a big deal. Always a little slow, he had taken three years to complete the two-year program. As usual, he was puppy friendly, eager to help.

"You want me to look up things? I'm good at looking up things."

"Good. I got a whole list. Herbert Overmeyer was murdered. And now Mrs. Brooks has been killed."

Jimmy shook his head. "Very sad."

"Yes, it is. And I'd like to find out more about it. I wonder if you could look on the Internet for me. Do you know how to Google?"

"Google? Sure, I can Google."

"Okay. If you could Google Herbert Overmeyer and Juliet Brooks. See how many hits you get. In the last three days. Can you look up the last three days?"

"I can do that."

"Here's a list of names. If you find any of these people mentioned in the same article as Herbert Overmeyer or Juliet Brooks, let me know."

Jimmy seemed disappointed. "Is that all?"

"No." Cora lowered her voice. "See if it says anything about murder."

"Gotcha!" Jimmy said.

Cora smiled as she watched Jimmy scurry off. He would surely find enough articles about the murders to keep him happy. But that wasn't what she wanted. Any mention of the heirs, however slight, would be a godsend.

Cora sat at a computer, Googled "robbery murder Mobile Alabama 1954." She got a thousand hits, none of them helpful. Most related to works of fiction. Some had "Mobile" and "murder." Some had "Mobile" and "1954." Some had "murder" and "1954." Some had "robbery" with some of those three.

Adding the name "Overmeyer" did nothing. The man hadn't been a suspect back then.

Cora plugged in the names of the witnesses who'd been shot, Claude Barnes and Mickey Dare, to no avail. None of the hits she got were promising. One suggested male enhancement techniques.

Jimmy came back crestfallen. He had gotten no hits Googling the list of names with Herbert Overmeyer or Juliet Brooks. He'd found all the recent *Bakerhaven Gazette* articles on the murders, but he must have realized they were things she already had.

Jimmy looked so pathetic that Cora wanted to give him another job, one he could succeed at. But she couldn't think of anything off the top of her head.

She fumbled in her purse for her cigarettes. She wasn't about to fire one up in the library, but she was damn well going to have one as soon as she got out the door. That was the worst thing about frustrations. They brought out all her bad habits. Next she'd be wanting a man.

Her hand hit something hard. The gun? No. Something rectangular. Cora pulled it out. It was a disposable camera. One she'd never gotten around to using.

"What's that?" Jimmy said.

Cora pressed the button. The light for the flash lit up.

She smiled, clicked it off. "This is for you, Jimmy. I have another job, if you wouldn't mind."

Jimmy's eyes were bright. "A job? Of course not. What do you need?"

"I want you to take pictures of all the heirs."

"The heirs?"

"The people on the list I gave you. They're Mr. Overmeyer's heirs. If you could take a picture of each one of them."

"The people on the list are all heirs?"

"Except Mr. Brooks. You can take his picture, too."

"Okay."

"After you take the pictures, drop the

camera off at the Fotomat and get them developed. Can you do that?"

"Sure. I've done it before."

"Here's twenty dollars. That should cover it. Keep the rest."

"Oh, I couldn't do that."

"I told you. It's a job."

Cora went outside and lit up. She felt guilty about giving Jimmy a bogus job, but she didn't have a real one. At least, not one he could do.

Damn it.

What was really bothering her was that she knew someone who could.

Cora stamped out her cigarette and went back into the police station, where Chief Harper was still holed up in his office, fending off the heirs.

Dan Finley was on the desk. He looked bored.

"Pretty slow day for a murder," Cora suggested.

"I'll say."

"Looks like you're stuck on the desk for a while."

" 'Fraid so."

"Gonna be here the rest of the afternoon?"

Dan frowned. "Why?"

Cora cocked her head. "Wanna run some stuff?"

CHAPTER 41

George Brooks's eyes were red and sunken. The police had let him back in his house, but he hadn't shaved, and his white shirt looked like the one he'd worn the night before. It had taken him a long time to answer the bell. Now he stood in the door-way as if he couldn't quite believe Cora was there.

"Mr. Brooks. We need to talk."

"No, we don't."

"Yes, we do. If you don't talk to me, you'll have to talk to the cops, and believe me, I'm better." Cora grimaced. "I didn't mean that the way it sounded. I mean I'll make it easier for you. You don't have to go into the station. Sit in the harsh room. Make a state-ment. Have it taken down."

"I did that."

"I know. It doesn't mean they won't be back. It's a homicide. It won't go away."

Brooks looked around miserably. "I've set

up shop in the study. I don't want to go upstairs."

"Did the police have you look at the room?"

"No. Why?"

"See if anything's out of place." Cora bit her lip. Everything she said was wrong. She wasn't usually so bad. Was it just that he was a handsome widower?

Brooks never noticed. He stood there, a dull expression on his face.

Cora took his arm, guided him into the living room. "Sit down," she said, taking over. She got him settled on the couch, sat next to him. "You've had a traumatic experience. You need help. Are you on any medication?"

"No."

"Do you have a therapist?"

"No."

"Did your wife?"

He turned on her sharply. Didn't answer.

"I don't mean to upset you, but it needs to be discussed. Did the police ask you that?"

He glared a moment, then turned away. "No."

"I didn't think so. And you didn't volunteer the information, did you? Look, I'm sorry to ask, but your wife had problems, didn't she?"

"Why do you say that?"

"Dennis Pride."

"Son of a bitch!"

Core nodded. "Yes. My niece's ex-husband has little to recommend him. But he talked to your wife. She told him things she never told the police."

"They never asked her."

"I imagine you didn't let them. Mr. Brooks, what your wife told Dennis is unusual, to say the least. It would be unusual to tell *anyone*. Which is why I'm wondering if your wife was under psychiatric care."

"You don't understand."

"I'm trying to. Can you help me out?"

He heaved a huge sigh. "Juliet had a stroke. Two years ago. Massive. Debilitating. She almost died. But she didn't. She recovered. Physically."

"I see."

"Do you? Mentally she had problems. Cause and effect. Impulse control. Simple reasoning." He shook his head. "I shouldn't have left her."

"Left her?"

"Alone. I thought she would be safe enough. In the country. No car. No way to get into trouble. I work in New York. I can't quit my job. But I shouldn't have gone." He grimaced. "Not with a murder next door. Not if someone killed the old man."

"If your wife *did* see someone in Overmeyer's cabin that night — if that man came back — would she have been afraid of him? Would she have locked the door?"

Brooks smiled sadly.

"She might have made him tea."

CHAPTER 42

Chief Harper drove his police cruiser up Cora's driveway, killed the engine, and got out.

A toy poodle erupted from the front door and, barking furiously, charged the lawman and circled him twice before darting off across the lawn.

"God, what was that?" Harper exclaimed.

"He likes you," Cora said. "Come in, Chief. He'll be back as soon as he overpees everything. You pierced his perimeter, and now he has to re-mark the property."

"Is that bad?"

"It keeps him out of the pool halls. Come on in, he'll be right along." Cora took Chief Harper in the front door, waited a moment to let Buddy scoot in behind. "In the kitchen, Chief. I gotta give him a biscuit or he'll never shut up."

Harper followed Cora into the kitchen, where she rewarded the little poodle with a puppy treat.

"Sit down, Chief, have a cup of coffee. I made a new batch."

Cora eyed the automatic-drip coffeemaker with suspicion. She knew it was one scoop of coffee per cup, or something like that, but she was never sure if it was level or heaping — or, for that matter, just which of several plastic scoops in the drawer was for the coffeemaker anyway.

Chief Harper regarded the cup of dark liquid she slid in front of him, wondered how long he could put off taking a sip. "You said to come on over. Anything the matter?"

"I just thought we should have a little talk."

"We've been talking all day."

"I thought we should talk here."

"Why?"

Cora poured herself a cup of coffee, added several teaspoons of sugar. "It's what we call home-field advantage."

"What?"

"I'm at a disadvantage in your office. You won't let me smoke, you make me chew gum, you're in charge, and you don't have to listen."

"You make me sound like a girl."

"Not at all. Like a police chief. Not

surprising, since that's what you are. Anyway, I thought we should have a talk without the jurisdictional restrictions."

"You're going to get me into trouble."

"Relax, Chief. You're *already* in trouble. You got two murders you can't solve, and you're being sued for every cent you're worth. You've hit rock bottom. Anything's bound to be an improvement."

Harper sipped the coffee, managed not to make a face. "Okay, it's your show. What'd you want to say?"

"I've got a problem with these murders. Not the same problem you've got, but a problem nonetheless. The problem is there's too much evidence."

"Are you kidding me? The problem is there's not enough."

"Whatever." Cora sipped her coffee. Grimaced. "Aw, hell. I don't see why making coffee's so hard, but it is. All right, will you take motives? There's too many possible motives. One, monetary gain. Which would make all the heirs suspects if it weren't for the fact there's nothing to inherit. On the other hand, the phrase *worthless property* always makes me suspicious. I immediately envision oil wells on Overmeyer's land. Huge derricks rising up and obscuring Mr. Brooks's view, yet another

254

motive. Though why the oil should be under Overmeyer's land and not Brooks is hard to fathom."

"This isn't oil country."

"No kidding. That's just an example."

"It's a bad one."

"Granted. But say that something makes the property valuable. The highway's going through, they'd have to buy Overmeyer out."

"What highway? That's an even worse example."

"Wouldja believe uranium?"

"Cora."

"All right, forget the specific example. The point is, it's valuable, one of these morons knows it, and that's what this is all about."

"You have one shred of evidence to indicate that's the case?"

"Just circumstantial. Someone poisoned Overmeyer, and all these guys turned up to inherit. That would tend to indicate there was something worth having."

"I don't like it."

"I know you don't. That's why we're playing in my ballpark. So we can discuss my theories whether you like 'em or not."

"I hate that one."

"Your displeasure is noted."

"What else are you serving?" Harper put

up his hand quickly. "I mean in terms of theories."

"Actually, Chief, I have a box of cookies from Trader Joe's I've been saving. If anyone deserves 'em, it's you."

Cora opened a box, poured some out on a plate. "Here you go. Butter Almond Thins. They make the coffee almost bearable."

Harper took one tentatively, was pleasantly surprised. "Thanks. You have any theories about this crime that don't involve Overmeyer's property being priceless?"

"Sure. First we got the gun. Big problem with the gun. You can't have a gun in a story without having it mean something. Of course, that's fiction. In real life you can throw in an irrelevant gun, no one will say boo. So maybe he just had a gun."

"He didn't *just* have a gun. He had a gun that killed someone in an armed robbery."

"Exactly, and that should mean something. If Overmeyer was about to 'fess up before he died, his accomplice could have poisoned him to shut him up. The Geezer is just about the right age to be that accomplice, and it would make for a very neat solution, if it weren't for the fact that the accomplice is dead."

"Do we know that for sure?"

"We certainly do. He's not only merely

dead, he's really most sincerely dead."

"What?"

"Come on, Chief. You've got kids. *The Wizard of Oz.*"

"I've got one daughter, and she's grown."

"So? I've never had kids, and *I* know *The Wizard of Oz.*"

"Just 'cause the guy is dead doesn't mean he was the accomplice. What if someone else was the accomplice?"

"I like the way you think, Chief. That's the first thing that occurred to me. Suppose Rudy Clemson, who died last year in Georgia —"

"Who?"

"Overmeyer's buddy. Suppose he's *not* the same dude who served with him in Korea, and was invalided out with shrapnel in his hip."

Harper's eyes widened. "You're saying he *was* because of the shrapnel?"

"No, I'm saying he was because of the death certificate. Not to mention the fingerprints."

"Fingerprints? What fingerprints?"

"Rudy Clemson, who died in Georgia with no means of identification. They ran his fingerprints to find out who he was. And guess what?"

"I have no idea," Harper said irritably. "I

suppose you're going to tell me."

"The man had a prior. A series of them, actually. Outstanding warrants dating all the way back to 1953. Right after he got out of the Veterans Hospital. Apparently suffering from post-traumatic stress syndrome. Popular with Vietnam vets, but I bet Korean War vets had it, too. He threatened his wife with a gun. Actually fired a shot or two. Took off on the road with guess who?"

"Was this just before the armed robbery?"

"Not *just* before, but a couple of weeks."

"On that you base the fact he was with Overmeyer at the time of the stickup?"

"Absolutely."

"Seems like there's wiggle room."

"Then there's the witness."

"Oh?"

"Mickey Dare. The bystander. The one who survived the shooting. He saw the two guys plain as day, gave a perfectly good description. It's in your notes, Chief. Didn't you look?"

Harper scowled. "I don't care whose ballpark we're in, my nerves are pretty raw just now."

"Sorry. Mickey Dare's description of the guy who shot him matches Overmeyer. Actually, it matches just about anybody. But the guy *with* Overmeyer. The accomplice.

The one who didn't shoot him." Cora smiled. "Had a stiff leg. Walked with a bad limp. Like a guy with a pin in his leg."

Harper gaped at her. "Where'd you get all this?"

"Went over to the library. Poked around. Amazing what you can find in a library."

"A small-town Connecticut library?"

"They got computers."

"And you got all that from the library computer?"

"I may have asked Dan Finley to run a few traces."

"What!"

"You were busy, Chief. I know technically I should have asked you to ask Dan, but you had your hands full. And Dan was on the desk anyway. No reason he should just sit there."

"You figure because what you got helps, you had a right to do it?"

"Actually, what I got *doesn't* help. It's another dead end. Literally. Overmeyer's accomplice is dead. The Geezer isn't him. But it's certainly interesting background. Here's Overmeyer living here for years, everyone thinks he's a harmless old coot, and today he's an armed robber."

"And yet you think this has no bearing on the murder?"

"It may, but the answer isn't so simple. We don't have an obvious cause and effect that ties it up in a pretty little package. We have to keep sifting through the rubble."

"Such as?"

"The stock-pooling agreement. The one we can't find. The one my late night visitor — boy, that seems years ago — says Overmeyer and a bunch of cronies pooled some stock."

"He's a bank robber *and* a stockholder?"

"See what I mean by too many clues? Either would be sufficient, but we have both."

"Have you traced him yet?"

"Who?"

"Your late night visitor?"

"I haven't a thing to go on. You want to dust for fingerprints, that would be fine. As I say, that was some time ago. I haven't been careful about touching things."

"So you let the stock-pooling idea go?"

"Absolutely not. I've looked into it. I just haven't gotten anywhere. You know how many shares of Philip Morris stock were issued in 1955? People used to smoke back then. And guess what? You can't get a list of stockholders. At least *I* can't. Maybe you could, as chief of police. You're looking for a block of stock owned by four guys, one of whom was Overmeyer, pooled under a name of which we have no idea. The only thing that's going to help us is to find that stock-pooling agreement."

"You want to search the cabin *again?*"

Cora shook her head. "I don't think it's there."

"Where do you think it is?"

"I have no idea. And I have no idea how to find the guy who told me about it. In my opinion, if that stock option exists, the only way we're going to find it is if someone makes a move for it. Which isn't very likely, because under the circumstances, no one wants to show any interest."

"You're not cheering me up."

"Sorry. But it helps to state the situation. Even if the situation is unhelpful."

"Great. You got any more unhelpful situations to state?"

"Actually —"

"Oh, hell."

"Don't blame me, Chief. Talk to Barney Nathan. If she was killed between nine and ten, it wasn't by anyone who saw Dennis on the late news."

"Obviously."

"So the field's wide open. So are the motives. Supposedly, Mrs. Brooks saw the killer. But that's the gospel according to

Dennis. Not the type of thing you'd like to stake your life on. But what if she *didn't* see the killer? Or what if she did see the killer and was killed for some other reason entirely?"

"By the killer?"

"No. If the killer killed her, that would be why. If she was killed for some other reason, we're assuming someone else wanted her dead."

Harper looked pained. "You're saying we have two killers?"

"I know," Cora said glumly. "It's worse than the meaningless gun. When you've got two murders by two separate killers, the writer might as well start looking for a day job."

"You don't think that's what happened here?"

"I'm not ruling it out. More coffee, Chief?"

Harper suppressed a shudder. "Perhaps a cookie." He took a bite. "So what are you getting at?"

"I had a little talk with Mr. Brooks."

"When?"

"This afternoon. While you were busy with the heirs."

"Is there anything you *haven't* investigated?"

"I'm not really up on the Lindbergh kid-napping."

"What were you asking Brooks?"

"I'm trying to judge how much credence we should give Dennis Pride. It was hard to get him to talk about it, because he's very angry."

"Angry?"

Cora gave Chief Harper a rundown of her conversation with Mr. Brooks.

"So, if what you're saying is true, she may not have known what she saw."

"Exactly. But the killer wouldn't know that. The killer might be lying low, waiting for her to give the alarm. He can't believe it when she doesn't. Overmeyer's body is found, no one is suspicious, it's ruled a natural death. The killer thinks he's gotten away with it. Maybe the lady saw him, but so what?"

"Until you poke around and prove it was murder."

"Now you're saying Mrs. Brooks was my fault?"

"No, I'm just following your train of thought. Go on. What happens next?"

"Once the murder is announced, the killer waits for Mrs. Brooks to go to the police. Lo and behold, she doesn't. The killer wonders why. It happened in the past, she doesn't connect the fact it's the same night, but there's always a chance she might, so she's gotta go." Cora shook her head. "See, Chief? That's the type of logic trips you up."

"What type of logic?"

"Bad logic. No logic. Suspension of logic and replacement with wishful thinking. The killer decides the woman might pose a threat in the future by remembering something she hasn't remembered yet."

"The killer doesn't know she has problems. The killer thinks she's a genuine threat."

"Same objection. If she isn't a threat today, why is she a threat tomorrow?"

"I don't know."

"That's your stumbling block. If you can't figure that out, your theory doesn't fly."

"It's not my theory," Harper said irritably. "It's your theory."

"Right. You haven't *got* a theory."

"Cora."

"I'm not saying that's a bad thing. In this case, it's probably good. Because all theories are wrong, and can be immediately proven wrong, so embracing one only makes you look stupid." As Harper started to flare up, Cora said, "Once again, I am using the word *you* in a nonspecific way. It makes me look stupid, too. Or whoever is expressing a theory."

Harper put up his hand. "My head's hurting. Stop telling me what we haven't got. Tell me what we have."

"I told you. Too many extraneous facts. We got a missing computer. We got a stockpooling agreement. We got a gun used in a convenience store robbery. Which should mean something, only it isn't involved in either of our two murders. Instead, we got a poisoning and a throat cut."

"Which would indicate two murderers?"

"No. Merely two murder weapons. Not nearly as bad as two killers." Cora picked up her coffee cup, reconsidered, set it down again. "Anyway, we have to consider Mr. Brooks."

"Why?"

"Time of death, for one thing."

"He was in the city."

"So he says. Doesn't mean he was."

"He said he was out drinking with the boys."

"Yeah. And the boys will probably back him up on that. Until they find out there's a murder involved."

"Why are you pushing Brooks?"

"I told you. The time of death."

"What about it?"

"Mrs. Brooks was killed before Dennis Pride blabbed about her on TV. Which means she was killed by someone who didn't hear Dennis talking about her on TV."

"Obviously."

"Which blows the motive. You have to say to yourself, what if she wasn't killed because she was a witness to a crime?"

"Then you're back to two crimes happening next door to each other that are totally unconnected."

"I didn't say they were unconnected."

"You said she wasn't killed because she was a witness."

"Exactly. But if she was made to *look like* a witness."

"Are you saying . . . ?"

"Of course I am. Brooks wants to get rid of his wife. He knows he'll be the number one suspect. So he bumps off the guy next door, and makes it look like his wife was killed because she's a witness."

Harper frowned. "Would that work?"

"Hell, no. It's got holes in it you could drive a truck through. But take it as a premise, there might be something there."

"So you called on Mr. Brooks."

"I figured it would be nicer than hauling him down to the police station."

"And he is a handsome widower."

"Why, Chief Harper. I assure you, I never thought such a thing," Cora waffled. "At least not in connection with killing his wife. I try not to date men who do that. Such a bad precedent, don't you think?"

"And according to Mr. Brooks, his wife was brain-damaged from a stroke, and probably couldn't have ID'd anyone. Even if she had, it wouldn't have stood up in court. Of course, the killer wouldn't know that."

"No." Cora's eyes hardened. "But Dennis would. He went on TV anyway, bragged that he had a witness."

Harper's eyes blazed. "Moron."

"Easy, Chief. It's not good practice to speak ill of the opposing party in a lawsuit."

CHAPTER 43

Cora was having a bad dream. Old man Overmeyer was dead. And Bozo and Cruella were dancing over the body. And the Geezer was cackling maniacally. And the Hooker was trying to escape without paying. Or being paid, that wasn't quite clear. And Snively, the Cranky Banker, was making them all stay after class and write, "I will not cheat a relative again." And Cora was being sent up to the blackboard to solve a giant crossword puzzle that she couldn't solve, which was frustrating because she needed to be able to solve something, because nothing made any sense, not even when Mrs. Brooks ran around telling everyone exactly what happened, only no one would listen.

Cora was distracted by an irrelevant bell, which had to be irrelevant because it was so far away, and if it was relevant, it would be right there, loud enough to attract attention.

Cora sat up in bed. What was that noise?

She knew what it was. Somewhere in the house, a phone was ringing. Actually, phones were ringing in two places, the kitchen and the office. Neither was close enough to her bedroom to wake her up, but they were an unpleasant background noise, like a dentist's drill, which had to be stopped.

Cora flopped out of bed, stumbled down the hall to the office, and snatched up the phone.

"Yeah?" she growled.

"Miss Felton?"

"Yes."

"Do you know who this is?"

"You woke me out of a sound sleep."

"I'm sorry. Do you know who this is?"

Cora blinked, welcomed the return of her senses. "Yes."

"I need to see you."

"Now?"

"Yes."

"What time is it?"

"One-thirty."

"Oh." Cora took a breath. "I'm glad you called. I've been looking for you."

"I need to see you. Meet me at the Town Hall."

"You've gotta be kidding."

"I'm not kidding. I need to talk to you."

"You can tell me on the phone."

"No. It's gotta be in person."

Under normal circumstances, Cora would have gone into her you're-a-moron-tell-me-the-missing-piece-of-the-puzzle-before-you-get-killed rant. But she still didn't know who the guy was. If he hung up the phone, she'd have lost him. "Okay. When?"

"An hour from now. In front of the Town Hall."

"An *hour?*"

"Best I can do."

Cora hung up the phone. Considered calling Chief Harper. She'd get points for clueing him in, demerits for calling him after midnight. It would depend on what the guy had to say. If he had no more info than he'd originally given her, the meeting was worthless. Most meetings of the sort were. No, the only reason for calling the chief would be if she was in any danger. And she wasn't in any danger, not even at two in the morning, not with a fully loaded revolver in her purse.

It was fully loaded, wasn't it?

Cora fished out the gun, flipped open the cylinder, and spun it. Fully loaded. She knew it would be. If her worthless husband Melvin taught her one thing, it was always reload. She could never think of Melvin without remembering the advice fondly.

And wishing the gun were aimed at him.

Cora lit a cigarette and stumbled around the bedroom looking for her clothes.

CHAPTER 44

The Town Hall was dark. There was no one on the steps. No car parked out front. That was a subtle indication no one was there.

Of course, she was a few minutes early. Fifteen minutes, actually. Did that seem overeager?

Cora drove on by, took a left down a side street onto Old Oak Road, circled around, and came out on Main Street next to the vet. Buddy needed shots. They'd been sending Cora reminders. Since she always got the mail when she was coming home, not when she was going out, that wasn't much help. But she really should take him.

Cora drove down Main Street. A block from the Town Hall, she pulled off to the side and cut the lights.

Was she being paranoid? Or cautious?

Cora stuck her hand in her purse, gripped the gun.

Cautious. Definitely cautious. She wanted

to see the man before he saw her. She might be walking into a trap.

Absolutely not.

The man who called her was not dangerous.

She didn't want to one-up the man by coming last, she just didn't want to put herself one down by coming first. By making it too easy for him to feed her any more lies.

Assuming what he told her before were lies. Which she had no reason to assume. But why would he call her at one-thirty at night if it wasn't important? And how could it be important if he was just reiterating what he'd already said? No, it was important only if he was *contradicting* what he'd already said. If he was coming up with a *variation* on what he'd already said. Bringing up some point he'd deliberately withheld.

If she had to get that out of him, she had to play her cards right. An experienced poker player, Cora was used to disguising the value of her hand.

At the moment, her best play was lying low.

She checked her watch. Two-twenty. Time was just dragging on. She wished she could risk a smoke. She'd seen too many old movies where private eyes on stakeout blew their cover by lighting up. It would be just her luck to have that happen. Or to have her mystery caller turn out to be a private eye hired by the other side to keep tabs on her.

Worse still, he could turn out to be the killer. Who lured her here to do her in. Why, she had no idea. It wasn't as though she was about to solve the crime. Frankly, she didn't have a clue.

But the killer didn't have to know that. The killer might have left behind a broad trail that she simply wasn't following.

That was a depressing prospect. Getting killed *and* being dumb.

There was a full moon lighting up the Town Hall from the clock tower down to the steps. No one was there. No one was standing there, no one was hiding there. Someone could be inside the front door, but that would be a neat trick, because the Town Hall was locked.

Cora's mystery man would have to drive up, unless he suddenly appeared around the corner of the building. A possibility, but why he'd be waiting out back was hard to fathom. Unless he, too, didn't want to appear overeager. Could he be behind the Town Hall?

Cora looked at her watch. Two-thirty. Give

him a minute? Hell, no. She was on time. He was late.

Cora started the car, drove up to the Town Hall, parked with her headlights on the door. She switched off the engine, left on the lights, and got out. She walked casually in front of the headlights from one side of the building to the other.

Okay, schmuck. I'm here. Your move.

He didn't make it.

Cora waited impatiently while the time clicked over.

Two thirty-five.

Cora heaved a sigh. Much as she wanted to see the guy, she wasn't standing there all night. She'd give it a once-over, and she was out of there.

Cora started around the Town Hall. She didn't have a flashlight, but the moon was enough to assure her the back parking lot was empty.

Only it wasn't.

At the far corner of the building, a dark sedan was parked.

Cora sucked in her breath, reached for her gun.

Should she go back and get her car?

She should if the guy was driving off. But why would he? After coming all this way to see her. That made no sense. But why hang out in the parking lot? Was he all right?

Cora crept up on the car. It was empty. She tried the door, but it was locked. Likewise the passenger side.

She checked the license plate. The car was from New York. Presumably the driver couldn't be far. Unless the lot was a drop where people carpooled. Did that even make sense? Cora couldn't tell. She was beyond the point where sense was a real issue.

She continued around the edge of the building and stopped dead.

The man who had called on her at her house lay sprawled out on the ground. He had a look on his face. At first glance, Cora couldn't tell what it was. Then it clicked.

Surprise. The man was surprised about something.

Cora figured it was probably the fact that his throat had been cut.

CHAPTER 45

Chief Harper was too sleepy to hone his sarcasm, but he gave it his best shot. "So, you didn't wanna call me at one-thirty in the morning, you chose to call me at three."

"I found a corpse, Chief. It's hard to overlook a corpse."

"He wasn't a corpse at one-thirty in the morning."

"No. He was a voice on the phone."

"The voice of the man we've been looking for. The man connected with the stock-pooling agreement. And you didn't think that was important enough to pass along?"

"At one-thirty in the morning?"

"It might have saved his life."

"Yeah, but then we'd never know."

"What?"

"We'd never know it saved his life. Because he wouldn't be dead, so we wouldn't know he was *going* to be killed, so we wouldn't know we'd saved him from anything."

"Please. I haven't had my coffee."

"And you're not gonna, unless someone fetches some. Wanna ask Dan?"

Dan Finley and Sam Brogan were processing the crime scene, such as it was. They'd put up crime scene ribbons around the back of the parking lot, stretching from the victim's car to either end of the Town Hall. The body lay just outside that triangle, so they had to set up a traffic cone and make a rhombus.

Barney Nathan had pronounced the guy, and the ambulance was on the way. Dan and Sam were trying to get into the car. They weren't having much luck.

"Guy has to get killed three in the morning?" Sam said, grouchy as ever. "Doesn't anyone ever die in the afternoon?"

"I don't think he did it just to spite you," Cora said.

"He might as well have. I'm down to my last stick of gum." Sam popped it noisily.

Cora had visions of the crime scene going unprocessed if the officer had run out.

A crowd from the neighboring houses was slowly gathering. Harmon Overmeyer and Snively were among them. The Cranky Banker wore a blue bathrobe. Cora wondered if it concealed pin-striped pajamas. Three-piece pin-striped pajamas. Cora

278

remembered they were staying at bed-and-breakfasts, wondered if they were nearby. It would explain their presence. Otherwise, they had no reason to be there.

Unless one of them killed him.

Which didn't seem likely.

"Who is it?" the Cranky Banker demanded of no one in particular. Not surprisingly, he got no answer.

Harvey Beerbaum pushed his way through the crowd. The little cruciverbalist was animated for the time of night. "We got another murder?"

"Yes, we do."

"Any chance it's a suicide?"

"Guy had his throat slit."

"That rules it out?"

"Ever try to cut your own throat?"

"It can't be done?"

"Well, if you did, you'd have trouble getting rid of the razor."

"Oh."

"What are you doing here, Harvey?"

"I thought there might be a crossword puzzle."

"Oh?"

"Since there was with the other body, I thought there might be with this one."

"There doesn't seem to be."

"And there wasn't one with Mrs. Brooks's body?"

"No, Harvey."

"Chief Harper didn't call. I didn't know if that was because there wasn't a puzzle, or because he brought it to you."

"He didn't bring it to me."

"I'm sorry."

"Why?"

"For thinking that. I just feel like an outsider. It's nice to be involved."

"Yeah."

"What's the matter?"

"You don't live here, Harvey. You live on the other side of town."

"So?"

"How'd you know about the murder?"

Harvey's eyes widened. "You don't suspect *me* of the crime?"

"Of course not, Harvey. I'm just wondering how you heard."

"All right. I bribed Sam Brogan to tip me off."

"Sam? Why not Dan?"

"I tried Dan. Seems he's in the doghouse for one thing or another. He didn't want to take the risk. Sam was happy to oblige."

"Happy? Sam?"

Harvey giggled. "You're right. It's an oxymoron."

Cora waggled her finger. "Now, you be careful, Harvey Beerbaum, or I'll tell Sam you called him that."

"I'm going to take a look. Maybe there's something they haven't found."

Harvey pushed his way toward the crime scene ribbon. Cora turned her attention back to the gathering crowd.

The Hooker caught her eye. Cora didn't recognize her at first with her makeup off and her hair in rollers. "There you are. I'll tell you, since I can't tell him."

"Him?"

"What's-his-name. He's keeping us here because there's been a murder. But does he clear it up? No. There's another murder. And another murder. Things don't get better, they just get worse, and how long does he expect us to stay here, that's what I want to know."

Cora'd had it with the heirs. "Yeah. This guy getting killed is a real inconvenience." She pushed past her just to get away, slipped under the crime scene ribbon, joined Chief Harper.

"You can't be in here," Harper said.

"Why not?"

"Everyone will want to be."

"Phooey. You're the police chief. Tell 'em they can't. I came to warn you. There's heirs over there. Think you're coming up with corpses just to give 'em a hard time."

He shrugged. "That's only natural. You don't have to tell me that."

"I thought I should give you the heads-up."

"Yeah. What do you really want?"

"You're getting sharper, Chief. I can't put anything over on you."

"So what do you want?"

"What have you got on the dead man?"

"There's no wallet on the body. Which makes it look like a robbery."

"Yeah. And if you believe that . . ."

"Robbery or not, it's gone. Which makes the identification a little harder."

"I assume you had better luck with the car rental agency?"

"Actually, they're not so quick to pick up this time of night. Or so cooperative." Harper jerked his cell phone out of his pocket, punched in a number. "This is Chief Harper, Bakerhaven Police. I got a corpse with no ID in a rental car, and the New York agent won't give me the information. The guy thinks a rental agreement is like the seal of the confessional. You got an officer could go over and pound some sense into his head? I got enough problems without listing this one as a John Doe." He listened, said,

"Thanks," and hung up.

"You put on the tough-guy lingo for his benefit or mine?" Cora said.

"Huh? I wasn't aware I was doing it. I must be really frustrated. He gave you no indication of who he was?"

"Just that he was related to one of the guys in the stock-pooling agreement."

"He didn't say which guy?"

"That would certainly have helped."

"Yeah." Harper frowned. "Why don't you go home and get some sleep."

Cora arched her eyebrows. "I look that bad?"

"I didn't say that."

"Well, work on your people skills, Chief. You've been married too long. You don't tell a lady she should go get some sleep."

"I'll keep that in mind."

Chief Harper trudged in the direction of the body.

Cora ducked back under the crime scene ribbon. Maybe she should go home. She wondered what she looked like. She hadn't wondered before. Not until Chief Harper made the comment. Why was she wondering now? Was she that insecure? Asking him how long he'd been married. How long was it *since* she'd been married? Why was she thinking that now? Was it because Sherry was off on her honeymoon and she was home alone taking late night phone calls and rushing off at two in the morning to meet strange men?

Who wound up dead.

Maybe she should just go home.

Cora started around the Town Hall back toward her car. She was just about to leave when she saw someone on the edge of the crowd who shouldn't have been there.

Dennis Pride.

CHAPTER 46

Dennis jumped a mile and spun around to see who had just clamped a hand on his shoulder. "Oh, for goodness' sakes!" he said, recognizing Cora.

"What are you doing here?"

"Are you kidding? There's been another killing."

"How did you know?"

"Everybody knows. It's a small town."

"You don't live in it."

Dennis grinned. "Talk to your police chief. I'm not allowed to leave."

"You're not staying in town. You're staying in a motel. There's no reason you should be here."

"Oh, yeah? Look around you. You think these people all live within walking distance? There's cars arriving every minute."

"How did you hear?"

"None of your business."

"What?"

Dennis grinned. "I got a lawyer. I'm not supposed to say anything that might get me into trouble. I have to be very selective. I don't *know* what might get me into trouble."

Dennis pointed at a hunched figure on the steps of the Town Hall. It was the Geezer. He looked like a predatory bird waiting to swoop down on the spoils of the kill. "See that guy over there? He's staying in the same motel as me. Why don't you hassle him?"

Cora's eyes narrowed. "Did you follow him here?"

Dennis's smile was cunning. "Ah, I see how your mind goes. Clever, but wrong. I have no idea why he's here. Maybe he followed me."

"Are you going to tell me what you're doing here?"

"I already said I'm not going to."

"Fine. Be that way."

Cora turned around and marched back to find Chief Harper.

On the way, she spotted Mr. Brooks in the crowd. She hadn't seen him before. Hadn't known he was there. She was surprised he cared enough to come.

Cora ducked inside the crime scene ribbon, snagged the chief.

"Dennis is here."

"And you're telling me this because . . . ?"

"I thought you left him at the motel."

"He wasn't locked in it."

"I'm wondering how he wound up here."

"Why don't you ask him?"

"He won't tell me."

"Ah." Chief Harper smiled. "You're tattling on him. Dennis isn't playing fair?"

"He won't talk to me because I have no authority. He'll talk to you."

"I can't wait," Harper said. "One more piece of junk I have to plow through before I can go home." He raised his eyebrows. "I thought I sent *you* home."

"I ran into Dennis."

"And thought it was worth telling me about. Fine. If you see him again, send him to me and I'll grill him. That's just if you happen to see him. Don't go looking for him. It's not that important. Go home, get some rest. I'll talk to you tomorrow."

"Sure, Chief," Cora said, and went to find Dennis.

She wasn't exactly disobeying the chief, but she wasn't exactly obeying him, either. She just wanted to know what Dennis was up to. There were a number of ways to casually bump into him. Cora tried them all. None of them worked.

Dennis was gone.

CHAPTER 47

Cora woke up feeling she'd slept the day away. She hadn't. It was two in the afternoon, and there was still some day left. She'd have slept that away, too, if Buddy hadn't barked to go out. Her muttered characterization of him was only half-true: His mother was indeed a bitch, but he himself had been neutered.

Cora let out the dog, let in the dog, fed the dog, wondered why she ever had a dog.

She splashed water on her face, struggled into her clothes, and discovered she was out of cigarettes. Fifteen minutes later, she was stumbling into the nearest convenience store with a face as white as death. If any children had seen her, they would have been put off their morning Granville Grains Corn Toasties for life.

Cora hopped into the car, lit up, and wheezed her way into town.

Harper's eyes were twinkling when she

came in the door. "Get some sleep?"

"A little."

"Me too. Good thing there was nothing pressing."

"Well, what time did you get in?"

"Eight."

"So, you've been here most of the day. You must have accomplished a lot."

"Four cups of coffee, a corn muffin, and a cranberry scone."

"I knew I'd forgotten something," Cora said. "So far all I've had for breakfast is a cigarette. You want anything?"

"If I have more than two muffins, my wife will kill me."

"She doesn't have to know."

"Isn't that how your last marriage ended?"

"Yeah, but it wasn't muffins."

It was slim pickings that time of the afternoon, but Cora lucked into the last blueberry scone. She plopped it down on Chief Harper's desk along with a large coffee with cream and sugar.

"Okay," she said. "The world looks brighter. What have you got?"

"What makes you think I've got something?"

"If you hadn't, you wouldn't be needling me about sleeping late. So whaddya got?"

"Actually, not that much. We ID'd the

dead man. Preston Samuels, bartender from New York, trendy Upper East Side bar. Been there three years, steady, good worker, well liked, co-workers express usual shock, etc., etc." Harper took a breath. "As far as his relationship to Overmeyer, that's where we hit a stone wall. He's not related to Overmeyer, he's related to someone who had a business relationship with Overmeyer. You know how easy that is to trace? I've been on the phone with Philip Morris. I've been on the phone with stockbrokers. I've been on the phone with the Federal Trade Commission. I've called in so many political favors Bakerhaven better not need anything for the next twenty years. And as a result of all that, do you know what I found out?"

"Nothing?"

"Bingo, right on the button. I could have gone home, got as much sleep as you, and found out as much about Preston Samuels as I did sitting here."

"Don't beat yourself up, Chief. We don't know what the guy knew. There may have been nothing to get."

"There was something."

"Why?"

"Because he's dead."

"That's the obvious conclusion. It doesn't

have to be right."

"You think he was killed for no reason?"

"No. Not at all. I'm sure there was a reason. We just don't know enough to figure out what it was."

"What about the pooling agreement?"

"What about it?"

"What if he found it?"

Cora grimaced. "That only works if the killer is someone who benefits from the pooling agreement, but *doesn't* benefit from Preston Samuels *having* the pooling agreement."

"Who would that be?"

"I don't know that much about stock. According to my broker, I don't know *anything* about stock. But say the stock is now valuable. Say the person holding it doesn't want to share. Overmeyer demands an accounting, so he has to go. Enter Preston Samuels. The only living descendant of one of the other three members of the stock-pooling agreement. When he first came to me, he thought someone was bumping stockholders off, and he was afraid he was next. He got cold feet and left before he could tell me what it was all about. After the second murder, he's determined. He comes back to give me the straight dope. Only he's silenced before he can spill the beans."

"And you make fun of my B-movie dialogue."

"What's wrong with that scenario?"

"There's nothing wrong with that scenario. And where does Mrs. Brooks fit in?"

"Innocent bystander. Sees the first crime, and has to go."

"And where does Overmeyer's thirty-two-caliber revolver fit into it?"

"It doesn't. He was a bad guy, who happened to have a gun."

"Which happened to be a murder weapon?"

"It has a bad history, I must admit. But it doesn't have to be involved with his death."

"I don't like it."

"I hate it like hell. But we have to take the facts as they are." Cora nibbled her scone. "So, what did Dennis say?"

"Dennis?"

"Yeah. Last night."

"I never saw him. Did you send him to me?"

"No. Didn't see him."

"He must have left."

"Did you see him today?"

"No."

"You mean Dennis has disappeared?"

Harper exhaled. "Dennis is not a high priority at the moment. If he shows up, I'll have to deal with him. If he doesn't show up, I'd almost thank him."

"That's not what I hoped to hear, Chief. What about Mr. Brooks?"

"What about him?"

"He was at the crime scene last night."

"So?"

"Isn't that a little odd? That he'd come all the way down from his house? I mean, even assuming he was awake. Maybe he was troubled and couldn't sleep, but out driving? That's a little much. And I can't imagine anyone calling to tell him."

"He probably just heard the commotion."

Cora blinked. "Huh?"

"He wasn't comfortable staying at the crime scene. And he didn't want to go back to the motel. He booked a room at the Johnsons' B and B."

"I didn't know that."

"No reason you should."

"What about the heirs?"

"What about them?"

"They been around today?"

"As a matter of fact, they haven't."

"Isn't that odd?"

"Odd or not, it's a blessing."

"You think they left town?"

"No."

"Why not?"

"It would look suspicious. Running away from a murder investigation."

"Doesn't mean they wouldn't do it."

"Of course not. Just the thought of inheriting a piece of that priceless cabin."

"Who could resist," Cora said.

The door flew open, and Brenda Wallenstein burst in. Dennis Pride's wife, though small of stature, was solidly built. She could be a real spitfire if she wanted.

Apparently, she wanted. She thrust out her chin and demanded, "Where is he?"

"Dennis?" Chief Harper said.

It was an automatic response, and a dreadful mistake. Brenda reacted as if she were being mocked.

"Yes, of course I mean Dennis. Who the hell did you think I meant?"

"He's staying at a motel up the road."

"Because you won't let him leave town. I know. And was there ever anything more idiotic? I was just by the motel, and he's not there."

"He's out."

"Of course he's out. If he's not there, he must be out."

"Well, did you look —"

"He's not at the Country Kitchen. He's not at the Fruit Basket, or whatever you call it."

"The Wicker Basket."

"He's not there. He's not at his lawyer's. He's not at her place."

"You went by my house?"

"Of course I did. All the likely spots. And he's not there. He's not anywhere. And you're making him stay in town, and people are getting killed. He's got nothing to do with it. Nothing. And you know it. But you're keeping him here where he's in danger. Now he's nowhere to be found, and how do I know something hasn't happened to him?"

"Don't be silly," Chief Harper said.

"Oh, that's silly? You don't know who the killer is. The next person Dennis talks to could be him."

"I understand you're upset. But, believe me, Dennis is in no danger."

"Of course you'd take that attitude. He's suing you. Why should you lift a finger to help him?"

"I assure you, that's not the case."

"Is he suing you?"

"Yes."

"Are you helping him?"

"Ms. Wallenstein —"

"Mrs. Pride."

"Sorry. Mrs. Pride."

Brenda stuck out her chin. "So, where is he?"

CHAPTER 48

Dennis Pride sipped coffee from a paper cup and felt like a real PI. Except for the fact he'd been doing it for two hours and had to go to the bathroom. He wasn't sure how real PIs handled that. Particularly in midtown Manhattan, where there were no facilities whatsoever, even if he had the time to use them. But he couldn't because then he might lose his quarry, and he wouldn't know whether he had or not, and what would be the point?

The other thing bothering Dennis was his car. He'd had to put it in a garage. There was no standing in midtown, and the same cop had asked him to move on twice. What if the guy he was following was parked in a different garage?

There was a lot of PI stuff Dennis wasn't up on. He was a poor PI, just as he was a poor husband, a poor ex-husband, a poor front man for his band. But he was determined to prove himself in his ex-wife's eyes, a hopeless task.

Dennis was standing there, holding his coffee cup, teetering back and forth from one foot to another, and worrying about his garage, when George Brooks came out.

Dennis almost missed him. Not that he wasn't watching the door, but he was so used to people going in and out that the guy just didn't register. Brooks came walking right at him before he had a clue.

Dennis immediately fell all over himself, dropping the coffee cup, ducking into a doorway, and doing everything in his power to make himself conspicuous. Lucky for him Brooks was preoccupied. He went right by Dennis without giving him so much as a glance.

Brooks was heading for the garage where Dennis was parked. If Brooks was getting his car, Dennis could get his, too. In fact, since he'd parked after Brooks, they'd probably bring his car out first. Piece of cake.

Brooks went right on by the garage, headed for Times Square. Was he getting on the subway? Why should he take the subway if he had a car? It was five o'clock, work was over, he should be heading home.

Dennis followed Brooks down into the subway station. Brooks went straight to the turnstile. Luckily Dennis had a MetroCard, or Brooks might have gotten away while he bought one. Dennis sailed right through just ten yards behind.

Several subway lines converged at Times Square, so Brooks could be going anywhere. He chose the Broadway IRT No. 1 downtown. The train was packed, as it always was at rush hour. Dennis didn't want to go in the same door as Brooks and be plastered up against him, but if he went in the door at the end of the car, he might not see him get out.

Dennis chose the end door. He'd hop out at each station, hop back on if Brooks didn't get off.

This plan was immediately thwarted when the train stopped at 34th Street Penn Station and the doors opened on the other side of the car. Luckily, lots of people were getting out, and Dennis was able to push his way to the door, ascertain that Brooks was not one of them. Indeed, when the door closed, Dennis could see Brooks, who had crossed the car himself and was standing in a similar position by the center door.

Hopping on and off the train, Dennis followed Brooks to Sheridan Square, in the heart of Greenwich Village, where diagonal streets cut through everything and the intersection of 10th and 4th streets had blown more than one young mind.

Dennis hung back, followed Brooks to a brownstone on Charles Street. It was divided, as many town houses were, into several apartments. Brooks stepped up to a row of buttons, rang one, and was buzzed in.

So. What would a PI do now? Push random buttons until someone buzzed him in? No, the people he rang would open their apartment doors. What would he tell them?

It occurred to Dennis that he wasn't cut out for PI work.

He had just had that thought when Brooks appeared in the front window on the first floor.

Hot damn!

Now, if he could just figure out who Brooks came to see. Maybe the name was on the doorbell. If he could tell which one —

No need.

Talk about beginner's luck.

As Dennis watched, the owner of the apartment came into view.

CHAPTER 49

Becky Baldwin was doing her best not to look exasperated. It wasn't easy. She was clearly fed up with her client and would happily have pleaded him guilty to anything from jaywalking to treason, if it weren't apt to get her disbarred.

Dennis Pride looked smug. Cora knew the expression well. Her ex-husband Melvin had a similar smirk on his face moments before she knocked him on his keister with a roundhouse right she'd learned from her second husband, Henry. Cora could feel her fist clenching.

Chief Harper wasn't thrilled, either. He rubbed his forehead, narrowed his eyes. "Your client wishes to tell me something?"

Becky took a breath. Her smile was thin. "My client *doesn't* wish to tell you anything. My client wishes to shut up on advice of counsel. Because my client faces numerous stiff penalties in the event that he should violate any legal statute, technical or otherwise, or inadvertently reveal some infraction he might have committed."

"Then why is he here?" Chief Harper said coldly.

"He's here because he insists on it. And while I can advise him, I can't tie and gag him. At least not under the current guidelines of attorney-client privilege."

"What do you want, Dennis?" Cora said.

"Don't speak to my client, speak to me."

"Phooey. I'm not a cop. Chief Harper is. Send him out of the room."

"I'm not leaving the room," Harper said. "If your client has something to divulge, he better divulge it, and he better divulge it fast. I got a triple homicide here. My patience is wearing thin. I'm in no mood to play games."

"Neither am I," Becky said. "So, unless you'd like to promise immunity . . ."

"For what?"

"For anything that might be divulged."

"In your dreams."

Becky shrugged, shook her head. "You see the situation? Suppose my client had material evidence in a murder case?"

"Then he better spill it."

Becky raised one finger. "But suppose the means by which he obtained it violated a

302

police directive?"

"Directive?"

"Didn't you tell Dennis to remain in town?"

"Are you saying he didn't?"

"Absolutely not. You can quote me on that. I never, ever said anything about Dennis leaving town."

"Good thing you didn't. I'd have to arrest him."

"And we wouldn't want that," Becky said ironically. "So, let's suppose someone, we won't say who, went to Manhattan yesterday and staked out the office where Mr. Brooks, the husband of one of the decedents, was employed."

"What the hell did you do that for?"

"Don't answer that. We're not admitting Dennis did anything. We're playing what-if."

"I'll give you a what-if," Harper said. "What if I throw Dennis in jail and hold him as a material witness until he's good and ready to tell me what I want to know?"

Becky shook her head. "That would be a most unwise course of action for someone already facing a suit for aggravated assault."

Chief Harper gnashed his teeth.

Cora leapt into the fray. "Right, right. I understand. You're both horrible people.

You eat your young. You shouldn't be allowed in the same hemisphere. Now, I don't care if you wrap it in a hypothetical or put a diaper on it and send it out to play. What the hell is the new information?"

"I've been playing detective," Dennis said smugly.

Becky's voice was sharp. "Dennis."

"Hypothetically. I've been hypothetically playing detective. And guess what I hypothetically found?"

"Let me beat it out of him, Chief," Cora said. "After all, he's not suing me."

"Actually," Becky said, "Dennis is starting to remember things about Mrs. Brooks's front porch."

Cora waggled her finger. "Let's not get away from playing detective. You're saying Dennis staked out Mr. Brooks's office?"

"Hypothetically."

"And what did he hypothetically find?"

Dennis was too excited to wait for the hypothetical. "His girlfriend!" he said triumphantly. "After work he went straight to his girlfriend's apartment!"

CHAPTER 50

"Okay," Chief Harper said. "Here's the ground rules. You give another interview on TV, I don't care if you say hypothetical, I'll lock you up and throw away the key."

"Now, see here. I won't have you intimidating my client."

"Yes, you will. The last time he talked on TV someone died."

"But not because of me," Dennis said. "No, I won't shut up, Becky. He can't say things like that. Mrs. Brooks didn't die because of me. She was killed before the interview aired. That's not just my opinion. That's according to the medical examiner. Maybe I can't talk, but I don't have to sit here and listen to things that aren't true."

"My client talks too much, but his point is well taken. There seems to be no doubt the woman was killed before the interview."

"I hope *my* point is well taken," Harper said. "There's not going to be another one.

Another interview, I mean. If your client so much as smiles at a TV camera, the deal is off."

"What deal?"

"The deal we have right now that's keeping him out of jail."

"Once again, I note the ugly aroma of intimidation."

"Ugly aroma?" Cora said. "Good God, where'd you learn to practice law, Hell's Kitchen?"

"I don't believe this," Dennis said. "Here I hand you a killer on a silver platter, and all you do is bicker."

"You think Brooks is the killer?" Cora said.

"Of course he is. A married man with a lover on the side. He can't divorce his wife. She's mentally incompetent. So he has to kill her. He can't, because he'd be the number one suspect. More than likely he'll be the *only* suspect. In which case the police will investigate thoroughly — not just like they are now — and uncover the other woman, and it's bye, bye, baby. So what does he do? He makes her look like she's a witness to a crime."

"I thought she told you she *was* a witness to a crime."

"She wasn't a witness to anything. She saw someone in the cabin. I don't know how suggestible she was. Hubby may have put the idea in her head."

"So that she'd tell you?"

"So that she'd tell someone."

"Oh, poppycock!" Cora said.

Chief Harper frowned. "Excuse me?"

"Would you prefer 'hogwash'? We're in genteel company, so I'm trying to avoid the more pungent synonyms for 'nonsense.'"

"Why is that nonsense?" Dennis said defiantly.

"Well, let's see. Her husband kills her so it will look like she was killed because she was a witness to another murder, is that right?"

"Yes."

"How would anyone know she was a witness?"

"She told me."

"And how would he know that?"

"Huh?"

"If you hadn't run your mouth off on TV, how would hubby know she spilled the beans?"

"That's easy," Dennis said. "He called her."

"Oh?"

"To say he'd be late. Which I'm sure he was in the habit of doing. He called her from the office to say he'd be late, and asked her if anyone had been around. She told him about me. He asked her if she told me about the man in the cabin. He could ask her directly, because she wouldn't suspect anything, and it didn't matter what he told her because he was going to kill her." Dennis Pride's smile was mocking. "See? It's not so difficult when you think it out."

"So," Cora said. "Your theory is he tricked her into thinking she saw something she didn't?"

"Yeah. What's wrong with that?"

"So, she never did see anyone in Overmeyer's cabin?"

"Not necessarily, no. The husband made it up."

"So, when you went on television saying you'd uncovered a witness to the Overmeyer killing, that was a complete fabrication?"

"It wasn't a fabrication. That's what I was told."

"And you thought it was true?" When Dennis hesitated, Cora added, "Because if you didn't think it was true, you're guilty of a total fabrication."

"No, I thought it was true."

"You were duped?"

Dennis bristled at the word. "I was lied to."

"Forcefully and convincingly. By a person not legally competent."

"By a person programmed by her husband to tell such a lie. Come on, Cora. This is about a killing. Much as you'd like to make it about me."

"Really? I thought we were celebrating your effective detection skills. Never mind. So, Mr. Brooks made it look like his wife was a witness to disguise his motive for murder?"

"Of course."

"And the murder of Overmeyer was just a coincidence?"

"Not at all. He planned it."

"Oh. Brooks killed Overmeyer?"

"Sure."

"Why? What was his motive?"

"You said it yourself. To disguise his motive for killing his wife."

"So, he bumps off the old coot who lives next door, makes his wife believe she saw someone in his cabin, kills her as soon as she spreads the word. Voilà! The perfect crime!" Cora grimaced, shook her head. "Well, almost."

"What's wrong with it?"

"His idea was to make it look like his wife was a witness?"

"Of course."

"And that's why he bumped off Overmeyer?"

"Yes. Isn't it obvious?"

"Only if he's dumber than you are."

"Huh?"

Cora smiled. "He wants his wife to be a witness to a murder. He wants it so bad he *commits* a murder. Only thing is, he doesn't commit a murder so it *looks like* a murder, he commits a murder so it looks like *natural causes*. Hell, if I hadn't browbeaten Barney Nathan into doing an autopsy, no one ever would have *known* it was a murder."

"So, Mr. Brooks screwed up. Some killers aren't that bright."

"No, no, no, no. You can't have it both ways. He's either smart enough to set up this incredible complicated scheme to get rid of his wife, or he's dumb enough to blow it. You want to try him for murder on a theory like that? I'd just love to be the defense attorney handling the case. That'll probably be Becky, and I don't think she'll be too thrilled with your theory. Bit of a conflict of interest, having one client trying to convict another. Think you can handle it, Becky?"

"I can if the guy's got a retainer."

Dennis didn't look quite so cocky.

Cora sized him up with satisfaction. "Now, you got any more theories you'd like to advance before Chief Harper locks you up?"

Chapter 51

"You can't do that," Chief Harper said after Becky Baldwin had hustled off her client.

"Can't do what?" Cora said innocently.

"You can't threaten a witness with incarceration."

"Why not? The police do it all the time."

"You're not the police. I am. You can't go around saying I'm going to lock someone up. He has a lawyer. If she's any good at all, she won't take kindly to threats."

"Trashing Dennis is fun for everyone. It's practically the national pastime."

"Is any of what he said true?"

"Very little, I would think. Mr. Brooks probably does have a girlfriend. One he wanted to leave his wife for. The rest of it is a pipe dream."

"You certainly made it sound that way."

"You're not happy with my analysis?"

"There must be a way it works. I mean, just because it doesn't seem to work that way doesn't mean it doesn't work at all. I know you made it *sound* like it doesn't. I also know you're so good at twisting words, you could ridicule anything."

"I'm not sure that's a compliment."

"What I'm saying is, what if Brooks did kill his wife? Could you make a case for it? In spite of what you told Dennis. Can you make a case for the other side?"

"Sure."

"I figured you could. Let's hear it. Say Brooks is the murderer. How does that pan out?"

"Start with separate motives."

Chief Harper frowned. "I beg your pardon?"

"Two motives is so much better than two killers, don't you think? If you stick with one killer, I'll forgive you practically everything else."

"How does two motives work?"

"Not that bad, actually. Once you concede that someone's a killer, it's easy to imagine them doing the deed." Cora grimaced, waggled her hand. "I don't mean that as stupid as it sounds. What I mean is, once you've killed someone, it's easier the second time. I think there's a scene like that in the James Bond film where they show him starting out."

"Cora."

"Anyway, say Brooks kills Overmeyer. Not because he wants to kill his wife, but because he wants to kill Overmeyer. Overmeyer is spying on him, Overmeyer is a lousy neighbor, Overmeyer has bad breath, whatever. Overmeyer's cabin is an eyesore and he won't sell it. I think Brooks said something to that effect before his wife was killed."

"I think he did."

"The point is, say Overmeyer's worth killing for his own sake. So Brooks does it. For no other motive than wanting him dead."

"What about Mrs. Brooks seeing someone in the cabin?"

"Two ways that works. One, Dennis is partly right. Once I prove Overmeyer's death is a homicide, Brooks sees an opportunity to bump off his wife. She's very suggestible, and he primes her with the story he wants her to tell. That accomplishes two purposes. It makes her a witness who needs to be killed. *And,* it creates another killer. It paints the picture of someone in Overmeyer's cabin who is *not* Brooks who could have done the deed."

Harper frowned, thought that over. "What's the other way?"

"Brooks's wife actually did see him in

Overmeyer's cabin. He has to explain that away. Since she's very suggestible, he's able to convince her that she's mistaken when she thought it was him, it was actually someone else. Based on that, he realizes what a neat opportunity it would be to have that someone else silence her."

"Dennis didn't think of either of those."

"Dennis is slow on his feet. You can bet Becky Baldwin will come up with those theories, and a dozen more. Assuming she doesn't wind up representing Mr. Brooks."

"Keep going with your 'Brooks did it' theory. How does Preston Samuels fit in?"

"Who?"

"Your midnight visitor. Corpse number three."

"Oh. Not very well. He showed up before Mrs. Brooks bit the dust. Worried about stock pooling. Which ties him to Mrs. Brooks in no way whatsoever."

"So why would Brooks kill him?"

"Why indeed? Somehow he must have figured out Brooks was the killer."

"How?"

Cora grimaced. "That's hard to fathom, since in all likelihood Brooks *isn't* the killer."

"Say he was. Then Samuels found out how?"

"For one thing, he's looking for a stock-pooling agreement. Where would he be looking for it? Overmeyer's cabin. Say he's searching the place the same time Brooks is sneaking home to kill his wife. He sees the car come and go. After Mrs. Brooks is found dead, he puts two and two together. Tries a little blackmail. Brooks won't bite. So Samuels calls me to turn Brooks in. Brooks says, 'All right, all right, you called my bluff. I'll get you the money.' Samuels tells him Brooks better get to him before I do. Brooks does, only he hasn't got the money, he's got a straight razor, and he slashes Samuels's throat."

"You like that?"

"I hate it like hell. It makes the stock-pooling agreement irrelevant. Not to mention the convenience store gun."

"So how *do* you connect Preston Samuels?"

"Pretty much the same way. Only assuming Brooks *isn't* the killer. The real killer is seen by Mrs. Brooks and blackmailed by Preston Samuels. Which would fit in nicely if the killer was looking for a stock-pooling agreement. Or tying to keep Samuels from finding it."

"What about the computer and the gun?"

"The computer theory is based only on a computer nerd's analysis of a crossword

316

puzzle. Which may be totally off the wall, because he's the type of guy who sees computers in the clouds. Were they computer terms? Sure they were. On the other hand, what isn't? Is a mouse a rodent? Is Spam a luncheon meat?"

"You're saying there may not be a computer?"

"Exactly."

"But there *is* a gun. So how does that tie in?"

"I don't know. But if the money from a convenience store robbery purchased a block of stock . . ."

Chief Harper's eyes widened. "Say. That might do it."

"Oh, come on, Chief," Cora said. "I'm just throwing this stuff out at random. You don't have to buy into it."

"I got three murders. I like anything that ties them up."

"I can see where you would. But let's not grab the first theory down the pike."

"You got any others?"

"Oh, sure. The surviving convenience store victim — the one who didn't die —"

"I know what you mean by surviving."

"The one who recovered comes back to avenge himself on the guy who shot him."

"After fifty years?"

"He's slow to anger."

"Cora."

"That would make him the right age for the Geezer. Which would be nice, because we need a suspect. Besides Mr. Brooks."

"The Geezer wasn't here when the first murder happened."

"As far as we know. You could check his whereabouts."

"Come on. You already said the idea is ridiculous."

"Yes, but *all* the ideas are ridiculous. One of 'em's gotta be right."

"Yeah, but it doesn't have to be one we've heard so far."

"It almost certainly *isn't* one we've heard so far."

Harper frowned, rubbed his chin. "You got any theories about Dennis doing it?"

"Don't get me started."

CHAPTER 52

Brooks looked guilty. Of course, Brooks should have looked guilty. But was he guilty of murder or just cheating on his wife? Cora couldn't tell. She'd had husbands cheat on her, but none of them had killed her, so she really had no way to judge.

"You were less than candid when you spoke to us before," Cora said.

"I didn't lie."

"No, you didn't. But you didn't volunteer anything, either. Not that confessions of marital infidelity are high on anyone's list. Still, with one's wife killed, the matter is bound to come up."

"Damn it."

"Just a minute," Chief Harper put in. "Let's not let this degenerate into a fight. Mr. Brooks, it has been fairly well established that you were having an affair with a Sarah Finestein of Fifteen Charles Street. Do you wish to deny it?"

"This has nothing to do with —"

"Maybe not. Your wife has been killed. It has been suggested that you are having an extramarital affair. It would be far better to admit to it now than deny it and have it pulled out of you in court. It might, in fact, help you avoid court."

"Mr. Brooks," Cora said, "no one's suggesting you killed your wife. But once a motive is raised, it needs to be dealt with. It would be nice for all concerned if it was dealt with quickly and expediently and without involving the press."

Brooks said nothing, looked straight ahead.

"Here's a promise. If you killed your wife, we'll get you. If you didn't kill your wife, we want to help you. Anything you do to help us will help you. So, tell Chief Harper about your affair."

Brooks lowered his head, looked miserable.

Cora felt sorry for him. Had to remind herself she'd felt sorry for Melvin once upon a time.

"It just happened. It had been hard, taking care of my wife. Always exhausted, stressed out. And . . . well, she didn't like to be touched."

"Did she have a therapist?"

"Yes."

"Psychiatrist or physical therapist?"

"Psychiatrist. We tried a physical therapist, but, like I say, she didn't like to be touched."

"That must have been a financial drain."

Brooks looked up in anger. "Yes, it was hard. Yes, it cost a lot of money. Yes, it was physically and emotionally draining on me. But I loved my wife. I took care of her the best I could. I could never hurt her."

"You were at the Town Hall the other night," Cora said.

"Yes."

"Why?"

"I heard the commotion. I came out to see."

"Why did you care?"

"What?"

"Since your wife died, you've been grousing around barely conscious. You haven't paid attention to anything in days. Why'd you care enough to go look?"

"I heard voices. Woke me up. People in the B and B. And outside the window. Saying there'd been a killing. So I went to see."

"Why did you care?"

"I figured it was probably the same person who killed my wife."

Cora nodded. "Good answer."

CHAPTER 53

Cora Felton sat and stewed.

What was it all about?

Like she'd told Chief Harper, too many clues.

The computer. Why a computer? What was the connection between Overmeyer and a computer? Overmeyer never had a computer in his life.

The stock-pooling agreement? Overmeyer looked the least likely person to own stock. Well, that wasn't fair. The only time Cora saw him he was dead. Still, having searched his cabin, she could not imagine a less likely insider trader.

However, he must have something because of the heirs. You don't get that many heirs for nothing. When heirs show up, there's property. Whether it be a stock holding, or the proceeds from a convenience store robbery, or an oil well in the backyard that no one knew was there.

Cora wished Sherry and Aaron were back. She thought of calling them, but that wouldn't be fair. Disturbing them on their honeymoon. She'd already disturbed them once, about that stupid puzzle. The one that didn't mean anything. The *second* one that didn't mean anything. The first one didn't mean anything either. Stupid old man, leave a crossword by your body in case you get killed. Leave a second one behind a picture in your bedroom. And neither one means a thing? That's really annoying.

Even more annoying is the guy with the info on the stock-pooling agreement who gets killed before he could divulge it. If he weren't dead, Cora'd like to wring his neck. When will these morons ever learn? Didn't they ever read a murder mystery?

She considered making herself a cup of coffee. Shuddered at the thought. Maybe a cup of tea. She didn't want tea. She wanted a nice Scotch and soda. But there was no Scotch in the house. It was a while since she'd given up drinking. A while since she'd had the urge. She knew she had to fight it. Sherry'd been reluctant to go on her honeymoon, not wanting to leave her alone. Sherry'd never forgive herself if she came back and found her aunt had fallen off the wagon while she was gone.

Cora rubbed her head. What she needed was a deus ex machina, a theatrical device to fly in one of the Greek gods to tie up loose ends and send the audience home happy. That didn't seem likely. More likely some devil would swoop down and offer her a drink.

There came a knock on the door. Buddy went ballistic.

Cora frowned, slipped her gun out of her purse. It wasn't late, but she was living alone. "Except for you, Buddy," she amended, so as not to offend the toy poodle in case he could read her thoughts.

Cora went to the door and opened it.

It was Jimmy Potter, the librarian's son. He looked younger than his years.

"Is it too late? I didn't want to come too late. But I thought you'd want to know."

"It's not too late, Jimmy. What did you want to tell me?"

"I got the pictures. The ones you asked me to take. It took a while, because they didn't all want to do it. Of course, Mr. Brooks I understand, but some of the others weren't very nice."

"No, they're not. I should have warned you."

"It's okay. But I didn't get everybody. I got *almost* everybody. So I figured I should bring you what I got."

Cora took the photos out of the envelope, leafed through them. "Who didn't you get?"

"The old man. Mr. Goldman." Jimmy shook his head from side to side. "He said things that weren't very nice."

"I bet he did."

"Do you want me to try to take his picture again?"

"No, Jimmy. You did fine."

"Good. I wasn't sure if I should get the pictures printed or keep trying."

"You did the right thing."

Jimmy turned back in the doorway. "Oh. I know it wasn't what you wanted, but I got his bio."

"Whose bio?"

"The man who got killed. Not Mr. Overmeyer. The other one."

"The bartender?"

"Uh-huh. Preston Saumuels. I looked him up. He's an actor. A real one. On TV." Jimmy was impressed. "He's been on *Law and Order.*"

Cora smiled. Every actor in New York had been on *Law & Order.* So Preston Samuels was an actor. Of course he was. Most bartenders were actors. Just like most waiters. And most taxi drivers. Before they started wearing turbans and having names with no vowels. New York City was awash with actors. Just walk into any bar or restaurant, you could find —

Cora blinked.

Could it be that easy?

Jimmy walked down the path, got on his bike, and pedaled off. Cora had forgotten Jimmy didn't have a car. He had biked all the way out here just to give her the photos.

It occurred to her that Greek gods came in all packages.

Deus ex machina indeed.

CHAPTER 54

McCorly's Pub on Amsterdam Avenue was as Irish as you get, with shamrocks over the bar and Shane MacGowan and the Pogues on the jukebox. Cora found herself watching her feet for fear of stepping on a leprechaun.

The bartender had a green Mohawk. Cora wasn't sure if that was Irish or punk.

"What'll you have?" he said as Cora bellied up to the bar.

The words *gin and tonic* hovered on her lips. She bit them back, said, "Give me a Diet Coke."

The bartender filled a glass, stuck a lemon wedge on it, slid it in front of her. Cora figured that would set her back a few bucks.

"You hear about Preston?" she said.

He looked surprised. "You know him?"

"Oh, yes. He used to drop by my house."

The bartender sized Cora up, reevaluating his late co-worker as part-time gigolo. "Is that right?"

"Are you an actor, too?"

The guy practically swallowed his tongue. Clearly the poor young man thought he was being propositioned.

"I have some connections," Cora said. "Used to throw theater work his way."

The bartender was more uneasy than ever. Good Lord, everything she said was worse.

Cora bit the bullet. It pained her to say so, even if it wasn't true. "A sweet boy. His mother asked me to look out for him. I feel so bad for him."

The mother card saved her. Cora could see the bartender visibly relax.

"That's hardly your fault. Just an unfortunate accident."

"Accident?"

"Well, whatever you want to call it. I guess he was killed, but that's like accidental. Just a huge stroke of bad luck."

"Yeah," Cora said. "As if things weren't hard enough for an actor."

The bartender blinked. "Excuse me?"

Cora grimaced. What an awkward transition that was. She wondered if it was the proximity of the liquor that was distracting her, making her not herself.

"Oh, the hell with it," she said. "I'm trying to pump you for information, I just keep messing up."

The bartender blinked. "What?"

"I'm a private investigator. I'm looking into his death."

"You're not an actress? You look familiar."

"Aw, hell."

His eyes widened. "I've seen you on TV. In commercials. For breakfast food."

"Yeah. I hate it like hell, but it pays the rent."

"Tell me about it."

"Someone killed Preston and I don't want him to get away with it. I need your help."

"What for?"

"You ever bartend the same time as Preston? You know, work the same shift?"

"Sure. There's always two people on the bar. We worked a lot of the same shifts."

Cora reached in her drawstring purse, pulled out the photos Jimmy had taken of the heirs. She spread them out on the bar.

"Who are they? Circus freaks?"

"Look 'em over, will you?"

"Okay." The bartender scanned the photos.

"Seen any of them before?"

"I'd like to say yes."

"But . . . ?"

"The answer is no."

"That's what I figured."

"Sorry to disappoint you."

"Hey, it was a long shot."

"Yeah." The bartender cocked his head. "Who are those people?"

"I don't know." Cora picked up the photos, stuck them in her purse. "But they're greedy as hell."

CHAPTER 55

Cora sat in the living room and didn't drink. The fact there was no liquor in the house made it easier, but still. With Sherry and Aaron gone and no man in her life, she was lonely. All alone with a mystery that didn't add up. It was hard to take.

She couldn't shake the feeling that if Sherry were there, it would be different. Sherry had always been there for her. Solving the crossword puzzles. The fact that Sherry didn't interpret them, just solved them, didn't matter. It was just the fact that she did it. Sherry solved the puzzles, and then Cora would take over. It wasn't the same if Harvey solved the puzzle. Or if Sherry solved the puzzle halfway around the world and then faxed her the answer. At least, it didn't seem the same.

Maybe, Cora conceded, the reason it didn't seem the same was that there was nothing to find. The puzzles were extraneous. Held no clue.

Except to a computer nerd.

Now, why was that important?

Cora went into the kitchen and poured herself a glass of milk before realizing it was the same milk she had rejected days before. She really should pour it down the drain. But then she'd have an empty carton, and what did she do with that? Was it recyclable? If so, where did she put it?

God, things were complicated.

What with some computer nerd declaring a computer puzzle.

What if it wasn't? What if the guy had never distracted her in that manner? Sent her off searching for a computer that didn't exist? What would the puzzle mean then?

The poem, unfortunately, was meaning-less. The theme entry. That's what Sherry called it. The verse didn't mean a thing. Cora wondered what Sherry would think of that. As a constructor, she wouldn't think much. It was a puzzle she could never turn in to the paper. The theme entry was a nonsense poem, probably the best the guy could do.

It occurred to Cora, maybe it had started out as something else, but the guy couldn't fit the letters in. He was a poor constructor. That was entirely likely. Would Sherry be able to tell that? She knew everything there was to know about constructing. But so did Harvey, and he hadn't noticed. Hadn't said, "You know, the guy must have been trying to say something else." That sort of thinking was outside of Harvey Beerbaum's area of expertise. Sherry, on the other hand —

Cora grimaced. For God's sake, she could get along without Sherry. The rhyme was meaningless drivel, not because she hadn't unraveled it but because it was meaningless drivel. And no amount of scrutiny was going to make it anything else. Aaron and Sherry were on their honeymoon, and there was no reason to bother them. None.

Certainly not so late at night.

Only it wasn't that time of night.

What time was it in Kenya?

Cora had no idea. That was part of Sherry's instructions, wasn't it?

Cora went into the office, leafed through the stapled sheets.

There it was: http://www.timeanddate .com. The World Clock — Time Zone Converter.

Great. A Web site to find the difference between any two cities. Let's see. She just had to type in —

Wait a minute.

Sherry had appended in parentheses, "(If that's too much of a drag, just add seven)."

CHAPTER 56

Sherry and Aaron were having breakfast in the dining room tent of the Masai Mara game reserve lodge. It occurred to Sherry the word *tent* was misleading. True, it had open-air sides, but it had marble floors and lavish dining tables, with ornate tablecloths, fine china, cutlery, and platters piled high with eggs, pancakes, toast, and a variety of breakfast meats.

"No bacon this morning?" Aaron said, passing the platter.

"It's hard to eat bacon with warthogs trotting around on the lawn."

"You think they'd be offended?"

"Probably not. It's just the nagging suspicion this bacon might be one of them."

"Now you spoiled my breakfast," Aaron said.

Jonathan, their native guide, giggled. "Is not warthog."

"Are you sure?"

He grinned a mouthful of white teeth, heaped a pile of bacon on his plate. "See? I hate warthog."

"You've *had* warthog?" Sherry said.

"Yes. Tastes like chicken," he said, and giggled.

Other guides at the table joined in.

"Where are we going today?" Aaron asked.

Jonathan looked pleased. "Baby lions. We look for lion cubs."

Sherry's backpack buzzed. "Uh-oh."

"What's that?"

"I'm getting a text message. That can't be good."

"No, it can't. I don't care what it is, we're seeing lion cubs."

"Absolutely."

Sherry fished her international cell phone out of her backpack. "It's Cora."

"Don't tell me."

"She wants to know if she can fax me a puzzle."

"I knew it."

"Relax. How long can it take?"

"I'm not missing those lion cubs."

"Don't worry. I'll solve it when we get back."

"You promise?"

"That's what I'm text-messaging her. I'll solve it when we get back."

Sherry sent the message, poured some coffee. Nibbled some toast.

The phone vibrated.

"Now what?" Aaron said.

" 'It's already solved, I just want your input,' " Sherry read. She began typing.

"I can't win, can I," Aaron said.

"Do you ever?"

A monkey dangling from the flap of the tent seemed to be eyeing Sherry's cell phone.

"Serve you right if he steals it," Aaron said.

"Eat your breakfast."

"Eat yours."

"I am, I am," Sherry said. She made a show of eating a few bites of her eggs before getting up.

She went out to the alcove, where battery packs and computers and cameras were hooked up to charge.

At the end, a fax machine was clacking.

Sherry retrieved the puzzle, studied it on her way back.

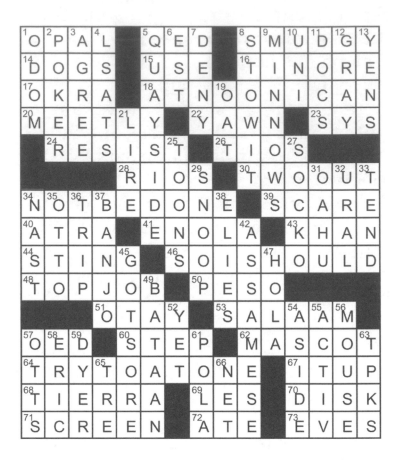

"Anything jump out at you?" Aaron said.

"You mean like a monkey?"

"I mean like anything you can tell Cora."

"Not really."

"Fine. Take it with you in the Jeep. You can read between the lions."

Sherry groaned, laughed, swiped at him playfully. She scanned the puzzle. Smiled. "You're right. Let's not let it ruin our day.

I'll just drop her a hint, and we can forget about it."

Aaron frowned. "You got it already?"

Sherry shrugged. "Not much to get."

"What is it?"

"Look."

Sherry typed in the message. Held it up for Aaron to see.

"How come it doesn't rhyme?"

CHAPTER 57

Cora stared at the puzzle and called Sherry names. Of all the nerve. She asks her for help, and what does she get? Nothing but cryptic nonsense, no better than the puzzle. "Why doesn't it rhyme?" indeed! It *did* rhyme: "At noon I can not be done. So I should try to at one." In what language didn't that rhyme? Maybe if you translated it into Swahili. Was that Sherry's problem? Too besotted by the safari, not to mention the honeymoon, to be able to think straight?

Even so, didn't Sherry realize she wouldn't be asking for help if she didn't need it? Here she was, half a world away, all alone, sorting out the last wishes of an insufferable little man who couldn't just say what he wanted — though not eating poison was probably fairly high on his list — a guy who bombards her with idiotic puzzles with meaningless rhymes, and —

Cora blinked.

A silly grin spread over her face.

How about that!

It *didn't* rhyme!

Sherry was right. Cora would have to make it up to her for all the horrible things she'd been thinking about her.

So, the puzzle didn't rhyme, and Overmeyer was a diabolical genius. Still a moron and a major pain in the fanny, but a diabolical genius nonetheless.

It occurred to Cora, damn, she should have asked Sherry if the puzzle had anything to do with computers. But that wouldn't work. If you ask someone to find computer clues, they'll *find* computer clues. The only true test is not to ask. Of course, then they don't know to look.

Cora knew to look. She was going over that puzzle from top to bottom. She picked it up, started in the upper-left-hand corner.

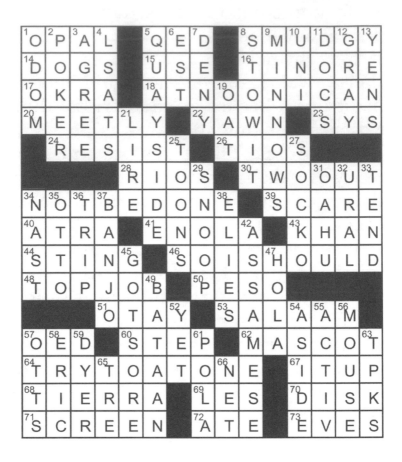

Okay, anything about computers there?

No, and —

Cora's mouth fell open.

Staring up at her from the puzzle were the words *poker* and *dogs*. And the second puzzle had been behind a picture of poker-playing dogs. The first puzzle was meant to send her to the second puzzle. The fact that the clue was so obscure that it hadn't worked didn't matter. It was clearly Over-meyer's intention. Luckily, Cora had uncovered the second puzzle on her own.

So. The first and second puzzles were linked. The first puzzle meant something. So the second puzzle should mean something, too. Sherry had figured out the secret of the first puzzle. But she'd solved the second puzzle without noticing anything special. She had no suggestions, no hint of any hidden meaning. Presumably, there was none.

And yet.

Cora picked up the second puzzle.

"Flip me over. Onto my back. Upside head. Take a whack."

Okay, Cora thought. That rhymed. And there was no way it meant anything else by not rhyming. So what about the verse itself?

It should be "upside *my* head." But she'd learned that Overmeyer wasn't too precise when it came to puzzles.

Or was he?

Was the lack of the word *my* a necessity of construction?

Or intentional?

"Flip me over. Onto my back."

Cora picked up the sheet of paper, turned it over.

```
. 9 .    . . .    . . .
5 . .    . . .    . 4 .
. 7 8    . . .    . . 6

. . .    . . .    . 5 .
. 3 .    . . 6    1 . .
. 1 .    . . 7    9 . 8

. 8 .    . 4 .    . . 7
. . 1    6 3 .    . . 5
. . 6    1 . .    2 . .
```

There were numbers scrawled on the back. Random numbers that could mean anything. She'd originally thought Overmeyer had done his puzzle on the back of a sheet of scratch paper. "Onto my back." But suppose the puzzle was on the front? "Flip me over onto my back." It would mean that the numbers were important. But they weren't. Just scattered random numbers.

Or were they?

Cora studied the back of the sheet.

Oh, my God!

She reached into the top drawer, took out a ruler and a pencil.

	9							
5							4	
	7	8						6
							5	
	3				6	1		
	1				7	9		8
	8			4				7
		1	6	3				5
		6	1			2		

Using the ruler as a straight edge, she began drawing lines.

A sudoku!

One good thing. If it was a sudoku, she knew how to solve it.

There was one way to find out.

If it was a sudoku, it would have a unique solution.

Cora snatched up the pencil.

Solved the puzzle.

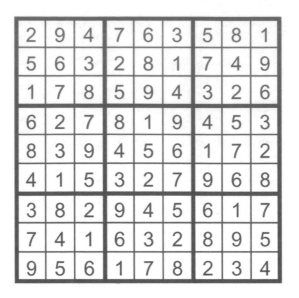

Okay. She'd solved the sudoku. So what? What could it possibly mean?

Nothing.

Unless you combined it with the verse from the crossword puzzle.

Okay, she'd flipped it over on its back. Now what?

"Upside head."

Head would be the first row.

But not the first row across.

The first row up and down.

The first column.

Down the first column?

No. Upside.

Up the first column the numbers read: 973 486 152.

What could that be?

Cora had no idea.

Well, great.

Instead of a meaningless puzzle, she now had a meaningless nine-digit number.

She turned the paper over onto its back or front or whatever, where the crossword puzzle was.

Cora scanned the puzzle, looking for another clue. But nothing jumped out at her the way *poker dogs* did. In the bottom left was *Mata Hari* and *I Spy,* certainly a theme, connected by the word *trap.* Had Overmeyer been involved in espionage and trapped by a cunning seductress? Somehow it seemed unlikely.

As Cora finished the second puzzle, something she told Becky Baldwin occurred to her. *When do you stop looking for something? When you find it.*

Cora had found *poker dogs* in the first puzzle and gone straight to the second. She hadn't finished going over the first puzzle.

She did so now. She picked it up, scanned the words.

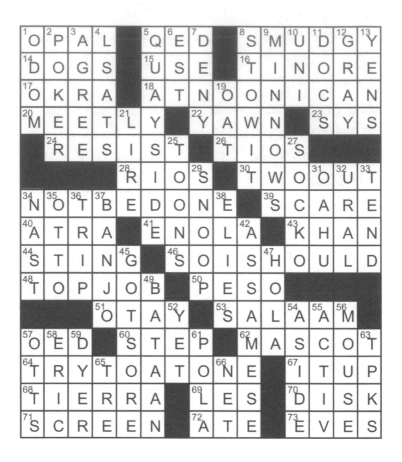

She found nothing until she got to the bottom of the page. The computer terms still looked like computer terms. But Cora knew they didn't have to be. The *screen* could be a window screen. A *mouse* could be the type that squeaks and eats cheese. A *net* could be a net to catch a *mouse* in. No, you didn't catch a *mouse* in a *net*. You caught a butterfly in a *net*. You caught —

Cora's eyes widened.

She snatched up the second puzzle.

There, at the bottom, connecting *Mata Hari* to *I Spy.*

Trap.

That infuriating little man.

You had to put the puzzles together.

Mousetrap.

CHAPTER 58

Cora killed the headlights down by the road. The last thing she needed was Brooks spotting her. If Brooks was even there. Had he returned home yet, or was he still at the B&B? With his lights out, it was impossible to tell. Was his car there? The top of the driveway was on the other side of the house. It didn't matter. She had to be quiet anyway for fear the neighbor to the north would hear her. Not that he was apt to, on the other side of the wood.

Cora's mind was racing, and she knew why. Because nothing made sense yet. Because all the facts she was amassing were a jumble of information that added up to nothing. Clues within clues within clues. Did this irritating man whom she had never met really mean for her to follow them? Or were they a figment of her imagination? Was she, like the computer nerd, duped into reading something into the puzzles that was not in fact there?

Did the first puzzle really refer her to the second? Poker-playing dogs indeed. So the words were in the puzzle. Big deal. There weren't even as many of them as there were computer clues. Why latch on to one and not the other?

Unfortunately, Cora had the answer. Because the computer did not exist.

And there *were* poker-playing dogs.

If the first puzzle sent her to the second puzzle, could the two puzzles, taken together, be sending her back here? In the dead of night? With a flashlight? Well, the flashlight and the dead of night had nothing to do with it. That was just when she figured it out. But could the puzzles want her to return to the cabin?

What else could they want?

Cora crept up the driveway in the dark, not wanting to risk the flashlight. She wondered if the front door was locked. Had the cabin been searched since she'd broken in? Sure it had. By every heir within a hundred miles. It should be locked up tight.

It was. The doorknob did not turn. Too bad. She wasn't really up for climbing in the dark. But there was no help for it.

Cora went around to the back of the house, pushed up the kitchen window. It wouldn't move. Someone had locked it, too.

Cora ascribed to the window private practices still illegal in some states. She fumbled in her purse, pulled out her gun, rammed the barrel through the windowpane just above the lock. She unlocked the window, pushed up the bottom. Brushed the glass off the sill and climbed through.

It wasn't easy. There was glass on the counter. Cora had to be careful where she put her hand. She wriggled through, squirmed across the counter, dropped to the floor.

She risked the light, shading the beam with her hand. Her fingers glowed red.

Cora crossed the kitchen, opened the basement door. She slipped in onto the top step, closed the door behind her. Took her hand off the beam and shone the light.

The basement was, as Chief Harper had described it, merely a crawl space. Cora, recalling what the chief had looked like when he emerged, wasn't keen on going down there, but there was no help for it. She crept down the three steps. She could feel the cobwebs clinging to her skin, smell the stench from the broken plumbing. She shuddered, pressed on. Reached the bottom.

The floor was loose dirt that gave beneath

her weight, creating the uneasy feeling that at any moment it might give way and plunge her into a bottomless pit. Cora gritted her teeth, shone the light.

There were the mousetraps she and Becky had found, arranged in a loose semicircle, curving away from the bottom of the stair. Leading to what?

There was nothing on the ground. Even the broken bike was outside the arc.

Cora raised the light.

The beam picked up the electrical wires Chief Harper had mentioned. Edison himself might have installed them.

Farther on was the shiny metal conduit of a heating duct. Installed in response to a building ordinance.

Stamped with a serial number, Chief Harper said.

Where would that be? Probably right at the joint. The pipe was joined by a two-inch metal strip wrapped around and fastened by a bolt and wing nut. There was printing on the pipe near the joint: "US Patent."

And the serial number.

973486152

Cora pulled the paper out of her pocket, compared the number.

Son of a bitch!

Her pulse raced.

Cora examined the joint. The bolt and wing nut were scratched, as if by a pliers and screwdriver. Someone had taken the pipe joint apart.

She didn't have a pliers and screwdriver. She took out her gun and began banging on the wing nut. The nut wouldn't budge. She began pounding the pipe itself, bending it in, away from the joint. It was rough going, because the crawl space wasn't high enough for her to stand. Cora sat on the floor, swinging the gun like a hammer. When she had the pipe bent enough, she raised her leg and kicked.

The pipe flew apart.

Something dropped out, fluttered to the dirt floor.

It was a piece of paper.

Cora picked it up, unfolded it.

It was a crossword puzzle.

Across

1 Megastars
6 French friend
10 "Gee!"
14 Bushes can be found here
15 Tailless cat
16 Utah ski center
17 Kayak user for thousands of years

18 Start of a message
20 Dryer fluff
21 Ziegfeld's nickname
22 Fleet of Spain, once
23 Pink, in a steak house
25 Et _____ (and others)
26 Rip off
29 "Seems I was wrong"
33 Part 2 of message
35 Classic Welles role
36 B&O stop
37 4:00 P.M., perhaps
40 "A mind _____ terrible thing to waste"
41 Highly diluted
43 Part 3 of message
45 Bookstore section
48 Idiot boxes
49 Concert hall section
50 C minor and others
51 "Likewise"
54 Smelly black stuff
55 Puts two and two together
59 Part 4 of message
61 Bashar Assad's land
62 Annapolis inst.
63 Bygone Mideast leader
64 Bad-guy role
65 Mason's wedge
66 Winston Churchill, e.g.

67   Beats by a hair

Down

1   Biased type, briefly
2   Cold cut store
3   Conestoga haulers
4   Toulouse-_____
5   Grounded flier
6   Go easy?
7   Lubricant for subs?
8   S&L earnings
9   Get rid of hot air
10 It could be a lifesaver
11 "The Three Sisters" sister
12 Ear piercer
13 1985 U.S. Open winner Mand-likova
19 Camera diaphragm
21 Member of la famille immédiate
24 _____ above the rest
25 Tax filer's dread
26 Punchers
27 Shop tool
28 Spam, for example
29 Advice to a sleepyhead
30 Easily fooled
31 Beginning
32 Glum drops
34 Jet black

38   Cut at a 45-degree angle
39   It's a sin
42   Bills, e.g.
44   Made an effort
46   Filly's foot
47   Diva, traditionally
50   "Misery" Oscar winner Bates
51   Hosp. areas
52   Child's portion?
53   All, as a prefix
54   The first one ruled 1547–84
56   Schlep
57   Jackknife, e.g.
58   Behaves like Simon
60   P, in Greece
61   That boat

CHAPTER 59

Harvey Beerbaum opened the front door in his pajamas and robe. He'd clearly been in a deep sleep and looked utterly bewildered.

"Cora! My God! What's happened?"

"Nothing, Harvey. I need your help."

"You need my help?"

"Yes, I need you to solve a puzzle."

"You need me to solve a puzzle?"

"If you're going to repeat everything I say, this is going to take a long time."

"What time is it?"

"It's puzzle time, Harvey. Are you going to ask me in?"

"I'm in my pajamas."

"Of course you are, Harvey. It's the middle of the night."

"What?"

"Harvey, trust me. I've lived through scandals in my day, and this doesn't measure up. The police could catch us doing crosswords at the kitchen table, and it wouldn't even rate the *National Enquirer*."

"*National Enquirer?*"

"You're doing it again, Harvey. Come on. You wanted in on the big time. Chief Harper brought you a puzzle. It was gibberish. I got one that may be the real deal. If it is, I'll give you credit. Come on, whaddya say?"

"You want me to solve a puzzle now?"

"At last, a meeting of the minds. Yes, Harvey, I want you to solve a puzzle now."

"Why?"

"Because Sherry and Aaron are chasing lions."

"What?"

"Wanna risk a light, or are you afraid the neighbors will know you've got company?"

"It's none of their business."

"Attaboy!"

Harvey flicked on the light. Cora swept ahead of him to the dining room table, sat in one of his rattan wicker-back chairs.

"Here you go, Harvey. It's a fifteen-by-fifteen. I'm giving you six minutes because you're not awake. Whaddya think?"

Cora spread the puzzle out on the table.

"Where did you get this?"

"I'm not at liberty to say."

His eyes widened. "Really?"

"Sound a little more interesting? Come on, let's solve this sucker."

Harvey got a pen, rested the puzzle on a magazine so as not to harm the tabletop.

"You do it in pen?"

"Of course. Don't you? Oh, that's right."

"Go on, Harvey, do your stuff."

With Cora watching, Harvey whizzed through the puzzle. He was done in four and a half minutes. While he was finishing up, she had already read the theme answer.

" 'By this gun I am cursed, but I never came first.' "

"Gun. What gun?"

"See, Harvey? Isn't that a little more interesting?"

"Do you know what it means?"

"Not yet. But I'm getting ideas."

CHAPTER 60

Chief Harper's voice was groggy. "Yeah?"

"I've got it!" Cora said.

"Got what?"

"A theory!"

Harper rolled over, looked at the clock. "You called me at three-thirty in the morning with a theory?"

"It's a good one."

"What is it?"

"I'm not sure."

Harper controlled himself with an effort, said, "Call me when you *are* sure."

"Okay, but you gotta do something for me first."

"What in the world are you talking about?"

"The convenience store robbery. The one Overmeyer had the gun for. That's what he was concerned with all along. Which is good, because if the gun wasn't involved, I was going to be mad."

"Cora."

"The witness who survived. Found lying on top of his buddy bleeding into a sewer drain."

"What about him?"

"First thing tomorrow morning, call the Alabama police and get 'em to pull that grating up."

"What?"

"It's a storm drain, right? A grate with a drain below? Have 'em pull up the grate and search the drain."

"You're kidding."

"No."

"It'll be full of water."

"So send a diver down."

"I don't mean like that. It'll be like ten feet deep with a foot of water in the bottom."

"So have someone climb down and search it."

"Why?"

"Because no one ever did," Cora said, and hung up.

CHAPTER 61

Chief Harper was madder than a wet hen. Cora had never actually seen a wet hen, but she figured they must be pretty mad to rate their own saying.

"I hope you know what you're doing," Harper said grumpily.

Cora plopped a paper bag on his desk. "Here."

"What's that?"

"Coffee and a muffin. Raisin bran. Great for a cranky old sourpuss. Straighten you right out."

"I don't know whether to thank you or arrest you."

"You call Alabama?"

"Yeah."

"And . . . ?"

"They weren't happy to hear from me. Imagine that. Would they mind climbing into a sewer drain on account of a fifty-year-old convenience store robbery? I don't know why they didn't jump at the chance."

"Did you remind them you have the gun used in the robbery?"

"Yeah. They were thrilled. Seein' as how the guy who owned it is dead. And his accomplice is dead. The case itself was dead until I opened it. Trust me, there's nothing cops like more than opening a fifty-year-old case they thought they'd never see again. A case they couldn't prosecute if they wanted to."

"Murder never outlaws. There's no statute of limitations."

"There is when the murderer is dead. Try and work up some enthusiasm for prosecuting the late Mr. Overmeyer."

"I can imagine."

"I got a police chief in Alabama doesn't think I'm the cat's meow. Thinks I'm a major pain in his fanny. For even *reminding* him of a fifty-year-old case. 'Take off a storm drain and climb down in a filthy sewer pipe? Thought you'd never ask.' "

"Drink your coffee, Chief."

"It's gonna take more than coffee and a muffin to make up for this one. I made the phone call on your assurance that I should. Without making you explain. Not that I *could* make you explain, but I mean insisting on it. All I know is you mumbled something that made no sense at all at three in the morning, and doesn't seem to make any more sense now. Since I did, you wanna give me some hint why I'm laying my reputation on the line?"

"I can't guarantee results, Chief. Fifty years is a long time."

"Now you tell me."

"But I'd never forgive myself if I didn't look."

"Are *you* wading around knee-deep in sewer water? You're not looking."

"You're not either."

"And don't think I won't be reminded of the fact."

The phone rang.

Harper scooped it up. "Harper here." He listened a moment. Blinked. "Are you kidding me? Give me that again. . . . No, I can't tell you why. I gotta do some checking on this end. . . . Because I don't *know* why. I'll put this together with what I got and see how it adds up. I'll get back to you as soon as I do."

Harper slammed down the phone.

"Alabama?" Cora said.

"Yeah."

"They take off the storm drain?"

"Yes, they did. And whadda you think they found?"

"A three fifty-seven Magnum."

Chief Harper's coffee cup stopped halfway to his mouth. "How the hell did you know that?"

Cora smiled.

"Some days you get lucky."

CHAPTER 62

Cora Felton twirled the gavel, smiled down from the bench. "We are here for the reading of the will. Becky Baldwin's law office is too small to accommodate everybody, so Judge Hobbs has been kind enough to loan us his courtroom.

"Please note that the media are here." Cora gestured to the Channel Eight News crew. Rick Reed's black eye had gone down. He had a Band-Aid on his chin, the little round kind that covers a shaving nick. "They may film if they're not intrusive. The minute they are, they're going out.

"Also note the presence of Chief Harper, who is here to maintain order. In the instance that some heir is not satisfied with what he or she gets, the chief will be happy to escort them to a holding area where they can think it through without disturbing the others. Because, in point of fact, this whole inheritance has dragged on too long. Understandable, give or take a murder or two. Still, with so many heirs forced to remain in town, the situation is sticky at best, and I'd love to get it resolved before anyone else is killed."

Cora looked them over. "To date, none of the heirs have been murdered. This is too bad. With an inheritance at stake, you'd think the heirs would want to bump each other off, in order to increase their cut. It's a nice clear motive. In Agatha Christie I think it's called a tontine. The survivors inherit more by voting the others off the island.

"One has already left. Miss Cindy Barrington." Cora read the name off a list to avoid calling her the Hooker. "She was seen boarding a bus. Which could mean she was the killer making good her escape, but in that case it's hard to see how she could have benefited from her crime. I think it's far more likely she was just a wannabe heir, throwing in the towel and abandoning a rather spurious claim."

Cora surveyed the remaining heirs. With the exception of Harmon Overmeyer, they looked decidedly uncomfortable.

"We're all here for the reading of the will. Except there *is* no will. Mr. Overmeyer died intestate. His property is to be divided amongst you. I am to do the dividing. I have been appointed Solomon. Mr. Overmeyer has trusted in my wisdom to see that the proper inheritance is distributed to the proper heirs."

"What do you mean, distributed?" Bozo demanded. "If there's no will, each of us has just as much claim as the other."

"Like hell," the Cranky Banker said. "You and your wife get one share. Just like everybody else. You don't get two."

"I don't see why not."

"This is something to take into account," Cora said. "The other consideration is what we do with Cindy's share."

"She left, she forfeited it," Cruella said spitefully.

"Who gets the cabin?" the Geezer demanded. "Surely we can't all get the cabin."

"No, you can't. You're virtually forced to sell it. And it's not going to bring much. It's a small piece of land with a ramshackle cabin. Whoever buys the cabin is going to have to demolish it, and no one is going to buy such a small piece of land if they have to do that. They'd buy undeveloped land and start fresh. Which means you have one buyer who can more or less dictate his own terms. Mr. Brooks would love to get that eyesore out of his sight lines. How much would he love to? I would imagine he'd make a reasonable, though not exorbitant, offer on the cabin, and wouldn't be inclined to raise it. Is that the situation, Mr. Brooks?"

Brooks heaved a sigh. "I don't know."

"Well, that's what you told Chief Harper."

"That was before my wife died. Now I might sell my place instead."

That statement set off a rumbling and grumbling from the heirs.

Cora banged the gavel. Smiled. "God, I like doing that. Now, if we could have no more of this. That answer may not please you, but it's certainly an answer. Mr. Brooks can sell his place if he wants. In which case he won't buy the cabin, and you get squat. I'm sorry, but this meeting isn't to make people happy, it's to sort things out."

"What about the other neighbor?" the Cranky Banker demanded.

"The neighbor on the north side is Mr. Arlington. There's a forest grove between the cabin and his house. He can't even see the cabin. The forest is all on his land, so no one can develop it. As far as he's concerned, the cabin might as well not exist. And he's not going to buy it just to upgrade the neighborhood. Is that your position, Mr. Arlington? You didn't kill Mr. Overmeyer just because he was a lousy neighbor?"

Mr. Arlington was an outdoorsy type, in a fisherman's vest and hat. "As I told the police, I have no interest in the case."

"I quite agree. You have no motive at all, and could care less about any of this. In a murder mystery, that would make you the most likely suspect."

"Hang on," Cranky Banker said. "If there's no will, how do we inherit?"

"I told you. It's entirely at my discretion. You get what I give you."

"That's not fair."

"I think you'll find it is. I think you'll find I am totally, almost scrupulously fair. I am, in fact, eager to dole out the inheritance. Let us clear the air. More to the point, let us clear the heirs. We have to deal with them first. Mr. Weston, stand up."

Bozo stood up.

"Here we are, ladies and gentlemen. Look at that. Do you see his red hair? Can't miss it, can you? And Mrs. Weston. Could you stand beside him?"

Cruella stood up.

"There you are. Straight out of the Addams Family. What a lovely couple. You have to ask yourself, Why in the world would anyone look like that?"

Cora spread her arms, looked around the

courtroom. "This is a toss-up question, anyone can answer, just buzz right in. . . . No one? . . . Okay. Well, here's the answer. Why would anyone want to look like that? Because they *don't.* They don't. And they don't want to be recognized for how they actually look. Because they're phony heirs, just hoping to cash in on the dead man's estate. That's why they look like they want to run. Okay, sit down, take it easy. No one's arresting you yet."

Cora twirled the gavel. "The thing that troubled me from the start is why are all these heirs in town? Particularly if some of them are bogus. To answer that, we have to look at the murders. I'll take the third one first. Like they used to do on the old quiz shows. 'I'll take the third part first, Jack.' Of course they were fixed." Cora grimaced. "Oh, hell, I just dated myself again. I was a wee slip of a girl, bouncing on my daddy's knee, had to have it explained to me. Where was I? Oh, yes. The third murder. Preston Samuels. Came to me right after the first murder was announced. Told me about a stock-pooling agreement, something a relative had been involved in with Overmeyer back near the dawn of time."

Cora looked around. "Why did he do that? Well, it served two purposes. One, it gave a reason for Overmeyer to be killed. Two, it created the impression of untold wealth and accounted for the presence of so many heirs."

She tapped the gavel into her palm. "Now, who would want to do that? Who would want a bunch of heirs traipsing around, falling all over themselves in the quest for untold millions? Who might have wanted a bunch of suspects on hand to mask his murder? You notice I say 'his' in the inclusive, nonsexist way that allows for the possibility of a woman, so that I don't have to keep saying 'he or she.'

"Now, who do we have on hand who is *not* an heir, who has a motive in the murders?

"We'll take the second murder next. Who had more motive to kill Mrs. Brooks than Mr. Brooks?"

George Brooks lunged to his feet.

"There he is now. About to protest his innocence. A totally pointless gesture, Mr. Brooks. That's exactly what you'd do if you were innocent *or* guilty. So don't waste your time."

"Damn it —"

"He's indignant. I've impugned his motives and insulted the memory of his wife. If he's banging a sweet young thing from

Greenwich Village, it's entirely coincidental."

Cora put up her hand like a traffic cop to stifle Brooks's indignant response. "Moving on. Anyone else have a motive that screams to high heaven? Yes. Harmon Overmeyer. The legitimate heir. He who will prevail when all others have fallen by the wayside. If he killed his great-uncle to get the cash, everything else could follow. Juliet Brooks sees him in the house, he has to silence her. For reasons of his own, he has to silence Preston Samuels. He got here before the other heirs, found himself alone, didn't like that situation, and saw that they were summoned.

"How did he do that? Perfectly easy. He posted Overmeyer's obit on the Internet. Which assured the arrival of professional heirs. Vultures who scan the obituaries for people who die with few or no relatives. 'Survived by his great-nephew' is a dead giveaway. No one's apt to be able to prove you're *not* related to the dear departed.

"So Harmon gets a bunch of scavengers here to mask his own movements in rifling the estate."

"Now see here —"

"Yes, yes, Mr. Overmeyer, we note your dissent. Like Mr. Brooks, you're innocent.

Give it a rest."

Cora stared him back into his seat.

"But why does he have to do that? Why rifle the estate if he's going to inherit anyway?"

Cora smiled. "Working backwards, we have reached the first murder. The murder of Overmeyer. Overmeyer died in possession of a gun used in a convenience store robbery in 1954. One might ask, why did he save a gun that long when it could incriminate him? But the fact is, he did, and with the discovery of the gun comes the implication that if Overmeyer was guilty of that robbery, he probably participated in several other related crimes. Which would eventually amass a goodly amount of cash.

"If the money were discovered as part of the estate, it would open speculation on the one hand, and involve a huge inheritance tax on the other. Which would explain why the heirs would want to eliminate the middleman and seize the cash before probate. Wouldn't that be the prudent course of action, Mr. Overmeyer?"

"I assure you —"

"That was a rhetorical question. Anyway, let's consider the decedent, Herbert Overmeyer. Did he have a reason for living like a hermit in his little cabin in the woods?

"Yes, he did.

"The convenience store robbery was a homicide. Actually, a double homicide. The proprietor was shot with a three fifty-seven Magnum. Two witnesses were shot with a thirty-two-caliber Smith and Wesson revolver. One of them died. Which makes each of the perpetrators guilty of murder, accessory to murder, murder in the commission of a felony, etc., etc., etc., lock 'em up and throw away the key.

"So it is not surprising to find Mr. Overmeyer keeping a rather low profile.

"So, what changed things?

"Overmeyer's partner in crime died. Rudy Clemson. He was a war buddy, been in Korea together, served in the same platoon. Got out of the army and hit the road.

"But not right away. Not before Rudy Clemson racked up an impressive string of felony arrests. After the last of which he skipped bail when faced with a likely ten to twenty-five.

"Anyway, he died.

"Overmeyer took it to heart. There is every indication that, as he saw his own life coming to an end, he felt the urge to clear his conscience and make amends. I have every reason to believe that if Overmeyer had lived, he had actually decided to confess."

Harmon Overmeyer sprang to his feet. "Oh, come on. If you're going to tell me his estate is ill-gotten gains and I have no title to it, I'm going to fight. You have no proof whatsoever."

"Actually, I do," Cora said. "Overmeyer left a clue behind. A crossword puzzle. Unfortunately, it was gibberish. A nonsense rhyme. 'At noon I can not be done. So I should try to at one.' Harvey Beerbaum solved it for Chief Harper. He understandably did not act on it. Why? Because it was meaningless. Harvey showed me the puzzle, and I quite agreed.

"Then Barney Nathan autopsied the body and discovered poison. At which point, I took another look at the puzzle. And had an epiphany.

"You ever read a sonnet? By Keats or Shelley or one of those boys?" Cora looked around at the sea of perplexed faces. Shrugged. "Yeah, I know. I prefer *American Idol* myself. I had to read 'em in college. And you know what? They cheated. They'd rhyme *glance* with *utterance*. Or *fiend* with *bend*. Even Shakespeare, in his most famous sonnet, 'Shall I compare thee to a summer's day,' rhymes *temperate* with *date*. Come on.

Just 'cause it ends in the same letters doesn't mean it rhymes."

Cora smiled. "See what I mean? Same thing with Mr. Overmeyer. 'At noon I can not be done. So I should try to at one.' No. The poem *doesn't* rhyme. The second line is 'So I should try to *atone*'."

Cora spread her arms. "So you see, judging by the crossword left by his body, there is every reason to believe that Overmeyer intended to confess to the crime."

The Geezer sprang to his feet. "Nonsense! That's a ridiculous leap of logic! There's no reason whatsoever to think such a thing!"

"Oh, but there is. Sit down, and I'll tell you how I know."

Cora waited for the Geezer to subside.

"The key to the whole thing was Overmeyer's partner. Rudy Clemson. Overmeyer was responsible for his safety. He was, in fact, the one thing standing between Rudy and prison. Nothing had ever connected either of them in any way with this convenience store robbery. And after such a long time, there was no reason to believe that anything ever would.

"Unless Overmeyer confessed.

"If Overmeyer confessed, it would be a simple job for the police to figure out who his accomplice was. Just as Chief Harper had no problem figuring it out once Over-meyer's connection to the crime was known. A confession by Overmeyer would essentially doom Rudy Clemson.

"Which is why he kept quiet until his partner died. Rudy Clemson died last year in Georgia. Why did Overmeyer wait so long to act? It probably took a while before he found out. The death of a derelict would not be front-page news. But once Over-meyer *did* find out, he immediately resolved to come clean. To go public with the secret that had been burning inside of him all these years. That would not let him rest or lead a normal life. That probably was the reason he lived alone, a virtual hermit in a run-down shack.

"Now, at last, he can tell his tale.

"And yet, he is killed before he can.

"How can that be?

"Who would know that he was going to confess? And who could possibly care? His accomplice is dead. His confession will close a fifty-year-old crime. He will live out the rest of his life in a solitary cell instead of a solitary cabin. No big deal for Mr. Over-meyer.

"Why is it a big deal for someone else?"

Cora picked up a paper. "Late last night Harvey Beerbaum and I solved *another* puzzle left by the late Mr. Overmeyer. Listen to this: 'By this gun I am cursed. But I never came first.' "

Cora looked up from the puzzle, grimaced. "Yeah, I know. Why couldn't the guy just say what he meant? Listen, everyone. While I have your attention. I am asking as a personal favor. If you ever find yourself in the position where someone is trying to kill you, if you want to let the authorities in on what's happening, *mention his name!* That's the type of clue the cops can really sink their teeth into. *The name of the killer.* Vastly underrated in situations of this sort. But, trust me, it's invaluable. If the police know who the killer is, they may not let him kill again. They're fussy that way."

Cora paused in her rant. Considered. "Where was I? Oh, yes. Interpreting the less than explicit message left by the late Mr. Overmeyer. 'By this gun I am cursed. But I never came first.' Is he blaming the *whole thing* on his accomplice? 'I didn't kill anybody, it was that nut job I was traveling with. Thank God he's finally dead, and I can tell you about it.' Was that how it was?"

Cora looked around at the baffled faces. "No. Obviously not. Why not? Because dead men don't bring poison. Sounds like a 1940s crime movie. Okay, if his accomplice didn't kill him, who did?

"There were four men at the convenience store that day. The two perpetrators, Overmeyer and Clemson. And the two witnesses Overmeyer shot, Claude Barnes and Mickey Dare. The one who lived, Mickey Dare, crawled across the parking lot to help his buddy, who was dead. The police found the two of them lying on a sewer drain. They revived one, and not the other.

"Early this morning, the Mobile, Alabama, police, acting on a tip from Chief Dale Harper, pulled up the grating, searched the drain, and discovered a three fifty-seven Magnum. We are still waiting on ballistics, but there is every reason to believe it will prove to be the gun that killed the convenience store owner. 'By this gun I am cursed. But I never came first.' "

Cora cocked her head. "Say you are robbing a convenience store. In the parking lot you encounter two men. They have heard the shots. They know you robbed the store. They are witnesses. So, what do you do? You shoot them. Simple enough."

Cora held up one finger. "Or it would be, if the witnesses are patsies. But say they're GIs. Soldiers home from the war who don't turn to jelly at the sight of a gun. Say one of them pulls a gun and fires back. Bad news for the robbers. One is shot dead. The other wounded, crippled, unable to escape. The jig is up. End of the road. Nothing can save him.

"And then, miracle of miracles! Instead of calling the cops, the two witnesses take off! Hop in their car and hightail it out of there!

"The robber can't believe it. It's like winning the lottery. He's been given one last chance.

"He crawls to his buddy. He pries the gun out of his fingers. The three fifty-seven Magnum with which he shot the store owner. He shoves it through the grating, drops it into the drain.

"The police find Mickey Dare collapsed and bleeding on top of his dead buddy. He tells a story of stumbling in on a robbery and getting shot for his trouble.

"Of course, Overmeyer knew he was lying. But Overmeyer couldn't come forward. Until his partner died.

"That's when Overmeyer contacted him. Offered to give him a chance to come clean before blowing the whistle. Well, Mickey Dare couldn't have that. Murder never outlaws. If Overmeyer talked, the guy was dead meat.

"So Overmeyer had to go.

"The killer called on Overmeyer at his

cabin under the guise of preparing to make a joint confession. Only the killer had no such intention. He slipped him a dose of poison and proceeded to ransack the cabin. Doubtless Overmeyer told him he had arranged for evidence to fall into the hands of the police if anything ever happened to him. He searched for it, never realizing it was in the crossword puzzle on the coffee table in front of him.

"Mrs. Brooks caught him at it and scared him off.

"She had seen his face. When it became clear Overmeyer had been killed, Juliet Brooks had to go.

"So did Preston Samuels, the actor hired to tell the stock-pooling story to attract the heirs. He'd also seen the killer's face, so he had to go.

"And who is the killer?" Cora looked out over the audience. "Jimmy Potter, stand up."

The librarian's son rose to his feet. Young, gawky, blinking. He was greeted by shocked gasps and a rumble of voices.

Cora banged the gavel. "Relax. I'm not accusing Jimmy. Jimmy Potter helped me solve the crime. At my request, he took pictures of George Brooks and all the heirs. Or almost all the heirs. Mr. Goldman declined to be photographed. Camera shy?"

The Geezer glared with contempt.

"I took these pictures to the bar where Preston Samuels worked. Showed them to one of the bartenders who worked his shift. Mr. Austin, would you stand up?"

The bartender rose from his seat.

"Would you remove your hat?"

The bartender took off his hat. His green Mohawk caused a murmur from the crowd.

"Mr. Austin, did you recognize any of the people in the pictures?"

"No, I did not."

"Of course not. If you had, solving this crime would have been easy. The killer would be someone who met Preston Samuels and arranged for him to tell his tale. But you didn't recognize any of them?"

"No."

"Now that you're here, I'd like you to take a look at the one man who refused to have his picture taken, the one man who is the right age to be Mickey Dare, and tell me if he is the man you saw talking to Preston Samuels shortly before his death."

The bartender nodded. "That's him all right."

The Geezer sprang from his chair, darted for the side door.

Sam Brogan rose to stop him.

The Geezer jerked a gun from his jacket,

aimed at the startled officer.

People screamed and scattered.

Dennis Pride nearly knocked Brenda down in his panic to get away.

A shot rang out.

The Geezer spun around, dropped to the floor.

Cora lowered her revolver. She resisted the urge to blow smoke from the muzzle.

She smiled wryly.

" 'By this gun I am cursed.' "

CHAPTER 63

Chief Harper didn't look all that happy.

"What's the matter, Chief?"

"The media is out there."

"So?"

"What am I going to tell them?"

"Well, for one thing, I shot the Geezer in self-defense and you're not pressing charges."

"I think we have enough witnesses you don't have to worry."

"Aside from that, tell 'em anything you like."

"I'd like to tell them something that made sense," Chief Harper said dryly.

"Well, you know about the robbery. Mickey Dare told a story, hoping it would hold up long enough for him to recover from his wounds and get away. He was surprised it not only did, but no one ever came forward to contradict it. Mickey Dare never knew who Overmeyer was. Figured the guy who shot him was long gone."

"Yeah, yeah, I know all that. Just give me a thumbnail sketch of what happened."

"Mickey Dare poisons Overmeyer, searches the cabin, is scared off by Mrs. Brooks. When Dennis Pride blabs that she's seen the killer's face, she has to go."

"Wait a minute. That TV interview was *after* she was killed."

"It *aired* after she was killed. That was Rick Reed, live on tape. You check up, you'll find the Geezer was there when it was *filmed*. Just *before* Mrs. Brooks was killed."

"Was he?"

"How the hell should I know? Just *say* he was. The guy's in no position to contradict you."

"Barney thinks he'll probably live."

"That's good. I'd hate to have to carve another notch on my six-gun."

"Come on, give me the rest of it."

"What else is there? Overmeyer told Micky Dare he'd left something that would implicate him. As insurance, so Mickey wouldn't kill him." Cora snorted. "And look how well that worked. Mickey just figured he'd find it. Only he's scared off by Mrs. Brooks. He has to come back. So he posts an obit on the Internet guaranteed to attract professional heirs.

"He also wants to create the illusion that Overmeyer had money and there was a motive for him to be killed. So he has an actor come see me about a stock-pooling agreement. Which is all well and good until he murders Mrs. Brooks. At which point the actor is a huge liability and has to go."

"Can the bartender identify him?"

"I doubt it. I told him to say, 'That's him all right,' whether he recognized the guy or not. It doesn't matter. It had the desired effect."

"How could it, if he was never in the bar?"

"You ever commit three murders, Chief? You're probably wound pretty tight. A guy points his finger at you, says, 'That's him all right,' you might not think too clearly."

"That may be hard to sell."

"Chief, it worked. You don't have to convince anyone. The Geezer's in the unhappy position of having to prove he wasn't there."

"And the crossword puzzle. 'By this gun I am cursed.' How the hell'd you find that?"

Cora knew the question was coming and was ready for it. "Once I knew the first puzzle said 'atone' I figured there must be another puzzle. When we searched the cabin, you commented on some newly installed heating duct. For Overmeyer, that seemed out of place. I pulled it apart, and there it was."

Harper frowned, thought that over. "I suppose."

"Cheer up, Chief. The case is solved. The TV people are going to love you."

"I'm still being sued for everything I own."

"Don't be silly. I had a little talk with Becky Baldwin. It seems her client violated probation by going to New York while under a police directive to stay put. I heard him say so, and I would be forced to testify to that effect in the event of a legal proceeding against you. In which case he would go to jail." Cora shrugged. "I think you'll find he's dropped the suit."

"Is that right?" Harper perked up. "Interesting." He cocked his head. "Is there anything else you're not telling me?"

Cora smiled. "God, I hope so."

CHAPTER 64

Sherry and Aaron cleared customs to find Cora waiting for them. They looked exhausted, but tanned and happy.

"Hi, kids. Still married?"

"Cora," Sherry said. "You didn't have to do this."

"Yes, I did. I should have gotten one of those little signs the drivers hold up: MR. AND MRS. GRANT."

"Oh, I'm taking *his* name now?" Sherry said.

"Don't worry," Aaron said. "Your professional name's still Carter."

"I don't *have* a professional name," Sherry protested. "*She's* my professional name."

"Good," Cora said. "If you're bickering like that, you must be still married. Not that I had any doubts. My marriages usually survived the honeymoon. If you don't count that annulment. And the case of mistaken identity."

"Mistaken identity?" Aaron said.

"She's trying to kid us out of it," Sherry said. "Don't fall for it."

"Fine. Let's keep bickering. What are we arguing about?"

"I don't remember."

"Damn. She's done it."

"How was Africa?"

"You wouldn't believe," Aaron said. "So many elephants you stop noticing them after a while. They're like wallpaper. And giraffes. And zebras. And some crocodiles. And all kinds of deer and antelope."

"Did they play?"

"Huh?"

"The deer and the antelope."

"Don't let her distract you," Sherry said.

"Did you take any pictures?"

"Loads of them."

"Yeah," Aaron said. "They're digital. We can show 'em on the TV."

"How the hell do you do that?"

Aaron launched into an explanation as they dragged their suitcases toward the short-term parking lot.

"So, how are things with you?" Sherry asked. "That hint I give you help any?"

"I'll say. You should have heard me explaining it in court."

"Court?" Aaron said.

"Actually, it was a probate hearing, but we did it in the courthouse."

"Of course."

"You'd have been proud of me. I Googled a bunch of poets and found some sonnets that didn't rhyme. I actually sounded like I knew what I was saying."

"Did you?"

"Are you kidding me? But I talked fast and no one noticed."

"Did the second puzzle help at all?" Sherry asked.

"What second puzzle?"

"The one I solved for you."

"I didn't tell anyone about the second puzzle. It was just too complicated, and it involved breaking and entering. After the chief told me not to do it again."

"Again?"

"I got caught with Becky Baldwin. Not her fault, but I claimed she was inventorying the estate for the heirs, which didn't fly too well when it turned out none of them hired her."

"Oops."

"No kidding. I didn't want to admit to going back. So I never told the chief about finding the second puzzle. Not to mention the sudoku."

"The sudoku?" Aaron said.

"I told you not to mention that. There was a sudoku on the back of the second puzzle, and all together it led me to the third puzzle, yada, yada. No one has to know how I got there. Chief Harper thinks there's only two puzzles and Harvey Beerbaum solved 'em both. Because I gave Harvey the first puzzle when it didn't matter, and I was too nice a guy not to give him the third one when it did."

"Huh?"

"Oh. And Harvey Beerbaum thinks I can't solve puzzles, I can only construct them."

"He's half-right."

"Yeah. Anyway, I'll show you the puzzles when we get home. They are the diabolic devising of a devious mind. If the guy weren't dead, I'd kill him."

"Never mind the puzzles," Aaron said. "What happened with the case?"

"It got a little complicated."

"I can imagine. So, what did *you* do?"

"Oh. I solved three murders, a fifty-year-old convenience store robbery, and shot a nonagenarian." Cora shrugged. "The usual."

The employees of Thorndike Press hope you have enjoyed this Large Print book. All our Thorndike, Wheeler, and Kennebec Large Print titles are designed for easy reading, and all our books are made to last. Other Thorndike Press Large Print books are available at your library, through selected bookstores, or directly from us.

For information about titles, please call:
  (800) 223-1244

or visit our Web site at:
  http://gale.cengage.com/thorndike

To share your comments, please write:
  Publisher
  Thorndike Press
  295 Kennedy Memorial Drive
  Waterville, ME 04901